His Brother Looked Human

Noel Stevens

iUniverse, Inc.
New York   Bloomington

His Brother Looked Human

iUniverse books may be ordered through booksellers or by contacting:

iUniverse
1663 Liberty Drive
Bloomington, IN 47403
www.iuniverse.com
1-800-Authors (1-800-288-4677)

Because of the dynamic nature of the Internet, any Web addresses or links contained in this book may have changed since publication and may no longer be valid. The views expressed in this work are solely those of the author and do not necessarily reflect the views of the publisher, and the publisher hereby disclaims any responsibility for them.

ISBN: 978-1-4502-2578-6 (sc)
ISBN: 978-1-4502-2579-3 (ebook)

Printed in the United States of America

iUniverse rev. date: 5/13/2010

Letter to Barbara from her brother –

"That husband of yours – Aldous – is the only man I envy. He is the epitome of today's hedonistic man; a modern playboy *par excellence*. He has what all we men want and can't have...

He'd never be out of the pages of HELLO if they knew about him."

Barbara, replying to her brother –

"Thanks for the warning. Men are the enemy all right, but let's not underestimate the limitless patience women have with the very rich ones."

KEYNOTE STATEMENT

Gulliver met the Aliens from the Unidentified Flying Objects, and they agreed that one day humans with deep space capability were a towering peril, very dangerous killers, a dread for higher planets everywhere.

HIS BROTHER *LOOKED* HUMAN

The airline wouldn't let him use a non-de-plume. His name, Aldous Windsor, went on to the passenger list, so the journalists and cameras were waiting at Heathrow.

"Mr. Windsor, do you have any predictions to make?"

Aldous smiled, and shook his head.

A girl with scraggly hair pushed a mike towards him and asked, "Will there be war in Kosovo?"

"It will all be settled quietly, if that is the exact word."

Faces fell.

"Trouble will be in East Timor."

They looked at him with open doubt and disappointment.

A girl with slick blonde hair stood beside her cameraman. Aldous asked her, "When did you last do a preggies test, my dear?"

She gasped, then whooped. "You're not serious!"

"Get on to it today."

"I can't believe it! I can't!"

A burly man with a mike, his cameraman right behind him, pushed forward and said, "Kosovo can't be settled that easily, Mr. Windsor."

Aldous smiled at him. "In September, don't go near any car. The whole month. Public transport for you."

His face collapsed in dismay.

"I can't manage without a car. No way."

"If you're dead, you won't have to," Aldous consoled him, and pushed his way through the crowd.

Aldous was six-foot-three, broad shouldered, blonde, with blue eyes, strong bones in his face and a prominent chin. Few women could resist him; they didn't try.

A very good-looking, photogenic photo-journalist, with lustrous dark hair and pouting lips said to him wickedly, "Can you help me in any way too – I mean, this of having a baby?"

He grinned. "You've caught me in an awful hurry," and shrugged slightly, his face remorseful.

1

He got through and went for a taxi.

* * *

At his London flat, on the third floor, he punched out the numbers on the plate to open his door. Then he had to wait sixty seconds, to punch out a second group, to switch off the beam inside of his door to sound the alarm at the police station. Inside the flat, he put his briefcase on the table and took out an electronic scanner to search for hidden mikes.

Aldous' income came from his three portfolio management companies, run by his three brothers. But he made a good income on the side from psychic readings. As he was domiciled in Jersey, in the Channel Islands, where one of his portfolio management companies operated, he didn't pay tax, so his psychic readings were black money, and his readings in this flat belonged to the black economy.

* * *

Fifteen minutes later, the doorbell rang, and he admitted an elderly couple, who greeted him with "Giddai".

They had written two months ago from Australia to make this appointment. They were coming on a trip to see Britain, but also to have a reading.

He sat them down, and the elderly man said, "We have a granddaughter of twelve, who is in a religious Home for Girls in Melbourne, where she is getting almost no education hut spends hours every day working in the Home's laundry. The Home takes in outside laundry... Our daughter got divorced from her first husband – the father of our granddaughter – ten years ago. She's an academic, and remarried, and had two children by her second husband. She tried to force her first husband to take the girl, hut he had remarried in Denmark and couldn't. So, out of revenge, she put the little girl in this place, two years ago. We have pleaded with our daughter to give us the girl, and she won't. So, if we go to Court, will we win?"

Aldous said, "I see a bad atmosphere for children's rights in Australia. I see bad attitudes. No, you will not, because legal technicalities have given your daughter legal custody. In four years time, your granddaughter, with your help, will demand her emancipation on her sixteenth birthday. She will escape from this nightmare Home and come to live with you both for eight years. Then she will marry a doctor who will take her to Sydney. You will move to Sydney, to be close to her, and she and her husband will look after you when you get very old."

2

"Thank you," said the lady, weeping quietly, with her handkerchief.

The husband took out his wallet. He said, with a catch in his voice, "How much do I owe you?"

"One hundred and twenty five pounds, please," said Aldous.

The Australian handed over the notes, and said, "You've saved us a small fortune in legal fees. We would have had to pay her lawyer and her costs as well."

He showed them out, then went back to his armchair and sat with his head in hands, rocking slowly.

What suffering...!

What was the point?

He felt an attack of anxiety coming over him, and pulled himself together. Pity and despair filled him for the girl in the Home – he probed gently, and then saw her face, and the whole layout of the laundry. He saw the religious supervisors, and their faces.

He wiped the image away, violently.

He felt rage for the daughter, and smothered it.

In the kitchen, he made himself a cup of tea, and drank it greedily. He would have liked a drop of whisky, but in a few minutes he had another appointment, a young man who was travelling from Derbyshire to see him,

* * *

Aldous showed him in. He looked about 22, dressed in jeans, dirty sneakers, and a badly crumpled thick cotton shirt.

On the phone he had told him the price, and that payment was in advance, and now he sat the young man down and waited.

He made no move to pay him.

Aldous probed the other s mind gently.

He didn't intend to pay!

Aldous took a deep breath, sat back tiredly, and said, "You find the price satisfactory?"

"Oh, sure."

"You remember I explained that payment was in advance?"

"Oh, sure. But how do I know whether it's worth it until I hear it?"

"Everything I tell you will happen exactly in that way. Of that have no doubt at all."

They sat in a silence that lengthened. Finally, the young man pulled out a brown envelope and handed it across. Aldous counted the notes, and nodded.

"It's like this, see. Everyone reckons I'm 22, but really I'm only sixteen and a half. I looks older than I am. Well, I met this girl who was hiking with

3

other girls, and. they came through our village and stopped at the pub for a drink. They was going to catch the train that evening for London, you understand? But this girl and me, we hit it off, and. as my parents were in Cyprus on a package tour holiday, I took her home and told her the house was mine. So, she spent the night, like, and she told me she was on the pill. We made love all night.

"She must have copied down the phone number, because now she's rung me to say she's expectin', and it's ours. She wants to come and live with me in 'my' house, except it's not my house, it belongs to my mum and dad. I've talked to 'em, and they paid for me to come and see you, because they don't want to have anything to do with another baby after bringing up myself and my brothers and sisters, unnerstan'?"

Aldous said, "She deliberately got herself with child because your house went to her head. She thought she would he guaranteed an entry to the house if she had your child. She will not have an abortion. The child will be given to State Care and will grow up in an Institution, when she learns your age, which you will tell her immediately. She will refuse adoption, not to lose contact with the child. It will be a boy, who will he poorly educated, will spend most of his life on unemployment relief and will die in an accident in his twenty-fourth year His mother will tell him who you are, hut he won't come looking for you because he will hate you too much. You will marry young, and push all of this into a recess of your mind. You will keep it forgotten, but it will affect your happiness and self-esteem without your knowing it. You will have four children, with your wife.

"You will always blame yourself, but she lied to you about the pill for completely selfish motives, and she will refuse an abortion or adoption again for completely selfish reasons, so while you have sinned, and that most definitely, you are more sinned against by far."

The boy was white-faced.

"That's it all, then?"

"You get on with your die-making," Aldous smiled.

"When I start working, she won't be after me for maintenance?"

"No, she won't. You heard me. Phone her, but put nothing in writing. Not a word in writing. Any question of papers or writing down something – you go straight to a lawyer. But it's not going to happen. You heard me. You'll be in trouble again with someone else – but when that happens, nothing in writing."

"What's going to happen?"

"I can't tell you because I can't see it clearly," lied Aldous. "All my powers are absorbed with this present predicament, and when that happens, I can't see other things."

"I must pay for another session?"

"Yes, but it's not worth it. It won't be anything as grave as this is."

4

He accompanied the boy to the door.

* * *

He looked out the window and saw a parked car.

His psychic eye told him they were detectives, watching his house.

He never paid taxes on his readings.

* * *

She was in her early thirties, dressed severely in a linen skirt and short-sleeved jacket, with a white linen blouse. Her hair was pulled back into a bun, showing a long, perfectly formed neck. Her face had high, classical bones.

Her movement of sitting was one of elegance. She crossed her hands demurely, and said, "I am engaged to get married, and we are talking about fixing the date. My husband is a businessman, a rugged sort, without too much subtlety. He has a square face, a square chin, square hands –" She laughed. "I'm trying to give you an idea."

Aldous could already see him, but she was giving Aldous her perception of the man, and he listened intently.

"Now, I was desperately in love for five years, but it broke up two years ago. Very painful. She was a marvellous woman, a full body, and she dominated me totally. I would almost swoon when I saw her naked...

"Which poses a big problem. Do I tell my husband about this? He's a very he-man type, and he dominates me, too, which I love. His body doesn't arouse any response in me at all, although I have orgasms making love to him."

She looked at Aldous thoughtfully.

"So do I tell him about my early love, or not?"

Aldous said without hesitation, "If you tell him, he will break off with you. Within three and a half years, when you are married and a mother, you will fall in love with another woman. He will never find out. When you refuse to leave your husband and child, the other woman will break with you. As she will often make you angry, the break-up will not upset you very much. In the eighth year of your marriage, you will fall in love with another woman, and while your husband will not find out, he will become suspicious, and hints dropped here and there will feed those suspicions. Your relationship with your husband will become stressful, conflictive. He will grow aggressive, and you will be unhappy at his loss of love towards you. You will put up with this until your child is fourteen, and then will seek a separation. You will win custody. That is what will happen if you marry him.

5

"You must understand that sometimes we see a clear future. Sometimes we see world lines, and which line will become actual depends on your choices."

"Do you know which choice I will finally make?"

"It would not be ethical for me to tell you that. You must be allowed to live your own life, to make your choices."

"And what other world lines do you see?"

"If you do not marry your fiancé?"

"Yes. If I do not marry him?"

"You will meet another woman, and form a permanent relation. In some years. First, you will fall in love with another woman, and it will not last."

"And no children?"

"No children."

"Is there a world line where I seek artificial impregnation?"

"Yes, with yet another woman. The choices are yours. You must live your own life."

"And what will the child be like?"

"An effeminate boy, with serious personality disorders. Your partner – dominating you both, you know?"

She stood gracefully, and with dignity paid him.

"You have been very patient, and I thank you for all you have told me."

She left silently.

Aldous had probed. The banknotes were not marked.

* * *

He went to the cabinet and got himself a small whisky, and sipped it slowly.

What waste! What suffering!

How did these things happen? How could he spare people this pain?

He couldn't.

So what was the sense of it all? Why, always, were people suffering? What sort of world *was* this?

He felt slightly sick to his stomach, thinking of the baby growing into a derelict, passing from unemployment benefit to SocSec, squatting where he could...

He caught the InterCity, which put him off at Arnside at four in the afternoon.

Arnside station had two concrete platforms, with bus-type plastic shelters, crowded in on both sides by trees and vegetation. No ticket office. It was one of the few tiny village stations in Britain where the InterCity and the great night Sleeper trains stopped, usually for a single passenger, as now.

He went outside and found no sign of Barbara or her car. He walked back into the station, and sat on the bench in the shelter, looking at the tree tops moving in the wind, and smelling the leaves. The July sky was clear and blue, with a few lost clouds gloating slowly across it. He was forty-five and had been unbelievably lucky. But why him? He could see that no threat faced him in the future. But all around him, people compounded their own misery, encompassed their own destruction, and when that didn't happen, other people did it for them. Ill-health, attacks from others, one's own mistakes... he had escaped, but he ached for others.

He paced up and down the immense platform, looking at the trees and the branches, then went outside the station and moved till he could enjoy the view.

In the distance he saw Barbara's car, and glanced at his watch, controlling his irritation.

* * *

He got in the car and went to kiss her. She turned her head, and took the kiss on the cheek.

Oh...

Barbara had a thin, triangular face, distinguished, but with fine lines growing around the eyes and mouth, the skin slightly dry and wind-burnt, her blonde hair tied hack. She put the car in gear and pulled away jerkily. She was edgy, and faintly antagonistic, and he said mildly, "You're late."

"Just as I got in the car, Mrs. Smyth came up with a story of how Eric had told her to be careful of burning her hand, and she had just had an accident and burnt two fingers. She said what a lovely, caring boy Eric was, and imagine a twelve-year-old guessing something like that. Fishing like mad, she was. I told her, you know what kids are like, full of ideas that haven't got much to do with the real world, and she went on and on, and the more impatient she saw I was, the more long-winded she got. I almost had to be rude."

Her undertone of aggression came through plainly. Aldous gently probed... and searched.

She had a new lover.

Aldous and Barbara were not married, hut they had three children, two girls and Eric, who was the eldest.

The new lover was... Jonathan. Twenty-seven. He lived in a Hall, with a high brick wall on the road, running hundreds of yards. He took... five minutes to finish making love. Aldous took twenty-five minutes. Barbara was exasperated, angry... but with Aldous, for showing up the younger man... she wanted to hurt, humiliate Aldous... she envied... was enraged and jealous at his long trips while she stayed in Edendale... his absences of three or four weeks...

Aldous leant back in the seat, and sighed.

Barbara turned sharply.

"What is it!" she exclaimed.

He lied smoothly. "What a pleasure to be on country roads after the cities and their filthy air."

They were driving along short country roads, lined with trees, whose upper branches and dense foliage met overhead to form green leafy tunnels.

* * *

He probed vigorously... Jonathan didn't have AIDS... He gave a prayer of relief. But Jonathan had another lover... and she didn't have AIDS... Barbara suspected the other woman but didn't know... she hated having to leave Jonathan for a week while Aldous was here... she was frightened of losing the young, wealthy... horseman... yes, horses... wait! wait!... they knew about it in the village! Barbara wanted to humiliate him but didn't dare, didn't dare let him know... she had to leave the village and live somewhere else... they all knew he'd have to steer clear of the lot of them. He grinned to himself, then broke into an outright laugh.

"What's the joke?" rasped Barbara.

"An investment that looked awful, and now the price is rising," he explained. "A bit complicated..."

Bloody Edendale...

* * *

Edendale was built around three sides of a huge square, with an enormous grassy sward in the middle. Hundreds of years ago, the houses had been all joined, no outside windows, only firing slits, one solid wall against the Scots, the border cattle raiders. The fourth side of the square had been a stone wall, with a high wooden gate, and all the cattle were driven in their hundreds into the central village green. Now the fourth side was open, with a dark brown, wooden bus shelter in the centre.

They drove up one side of the village green, across the top and halfway down the other side. Aldous got out and opened the high doors, and Barbara drove in beside the house, into the covered drive. She came out, Aldous closed the doors, and they went to the front door, climbing up stone steps.

Aldous glanced around the houses across the green, looking for a twitching curtain, but most of the windows were uncurtained, great expanses of shining glass you couldn't see behind. The neighbours would be watching, and he grinned again.

The house was two-storied, with bow windows above a high stone wall. The afternoon sunlight was white, tired, and cast a sad light. They went in the front door, set on one side, heavy, dark wood, highly varnished, and walked along the passage with the French wallpaper and prints, into the living-room. Thank God, the bow windows did have curtains, with the sunlight coming though them onto the comfortable, grey upholstered furniture.

"Where are the kids?"

"Playing in that copse near the church."

The church was hidden in a small valley, among thick trees, some hundreds of yards from the village, and over the centuries, the Border raiders never found it.

"Wonderful," said Aldous. "Let's make love."

He took her in his arms, and felt her tenseness, the hardness of her muscles.

"Aren't you horny! All you think about!" She wriggled free, and he probed.

...she wanted to, and despised herself for wanting two men at once...

He caught her again, and gently kneaded her tight back, and found her lips. She struggled and pushed, and then he heard the kitchen door.

"Dad!"

Aldous pulled away from Barbara, and Eric came running in and grabbed his father around the waist, holding his head against his chest.

"I 'felt' you and came running. I thought you'd never come home!"

Aldous embraced him tightly.

"More voices, son?" he asked. "They're not upsetting you?"

Eric was psychic, as was his ten-year-old sister Jocelyn.

"You told me it was all right, and now I enjoy them. They tell me what to do."

"And what do you have to do, might I ask?" said Aldous.

"We've got to go to Mountfoot, dad."

"Mountfoot!" cried his mother. "What is he talking about?"

She lived a life of upsets and starts with her psychic children.

"It's a house, mum. A beautiful house, all by itself. At the foot of the Pennines.

Barbara stiffened, and a half smile dawned. "A house by itself?"

Aldous said, "Quiet everyone. Let me think."

He concentrated, then saw the cottage. There was an estate agent sign outside, and he 'read' the address in Penrith.

"It s beautiful," said Aldous softly. "And why do we have to go there?"

"I'm being bullied all the time at school, and two of the chaps live here in the village. I'm fighting them all the time and I'm always losing. I don't want to do that. I want to study."

Barbara broke in. "Aldous, that's what I wanted to talk to you about, but I didn't know how to broach the subject, and as you're just off the train..."

"Go on, please", said Aldous calmly. "I'm listening."

"All right," said Barbara. "Let me give it to you. Eric is in trouble at school with these bullies, and Jocelyn is in trouble too with some 'visions' that have upset the teachers —"

Their two daughters came in from the kitchen.

Helen ran to him, eight years old, and he scooped her up and kissed her. He put her down and lifted up Jocelyn, and rubbed his face in hers.

"Oh, what a prickly beard," she cried delightedly.

"Whew," said Aldous, putting her down. "You're getting too big."

"You just ran off," said Jocelyn, furious at Eric. "You didn't tell us he was back."

"If you can't 'see' for yourself," said Eric loftily.

"No, I didn't 'see' him," cried Jocelyn. "We were playing. I would have told you, you beast."

"Stop it," said Barbara.

"Dad, we've got to leave here," pleaded Jocelyn. "I'm in awful trouble at school. Some Roundhead soldiers came into class and stood beside the teacher. They had pikes and you could see *dried blood* on them."

Aldous gaped.

"Did she see ghosts?" demanded Barbara.

"No, she didn't," muttered Aldous, confused and alarmed. "Let me think. Let me think! If there were ghosts, we'd have stories going back hundreds of years. But there's never a word, nary a word..."

They stood in silence, watching him, as he stared at the wall.

"I can't believe it. I can't. I've never heard anything remotely like it. Jocelyn can see into the past. It's amazing."

"That amazes me much less than being able to see into the future," said Barbara grimly. "Now this is something I can understand. Jocelyn, aren't you sensible!" She took Jocelyn and gave her a hug.

Jocelyn began crying.

"It caught me by surprise. I blurted it out. Now all the kids are laughing at me, and the teachers keep staring at me when they think I'm not watching."

She wept.

Aldous put his arm around her.

"Eric has just 'seen' a wonderful new house called Mountfoot."

Jocelyn stopped crying and looked at them hopefully.

Barbara said loudly, "I want everyone to stop talking this very minute and to listen. Silence!"

They all stopped at looked at her.

"That's better. Aldous, if we can find a cottage by itself somewhere, I can teach the children myself at home. There's a special Educational Authority for that, and they tell you what you have to teach, and they do the exams. That means that I can buy other books as well as the set books for the children to read. Usually, children taught at home like this do better than those in the schools."

"Don't the children need to develop social skills among their peers at school?"

"Bah! Blathering nonsense. They can socialise at University, where they are more civilised. I want to get the children out of this village and out of school as fast as we can."

Aldous asked innocently, "Don't you like your neighbours anymore?"

She snapped, "I don't. Not when they conflict with the interests of my children. If I have to make a sacrifice, there's no question about it."

"Virtue enthroned," said Aldous, picking up Helen. "So be it. Helen, take good note, for when you grow up."

"Daddy, what's all this talk? What's happening?" asked Helen, uncertain.

"My little girl, we're going to live in another house."

"But this is a lovely house. And does mummy have a throne? Where is it?"

"The throne is in mummy's heart," said Aldous.

He gave her a big hug, and put her down.

"The Estate Agent's in Penrith, and tomorrow morning I'll drive over there and get the keys, then come back here and pick up everyone to go and see it. The same agent can sell this house. We'll tell everyone we're going to London" – he looked around the children – "to London!" he repeated.

"How far away is this place?"

"Thirty miles, more or less. About half a mile from Flake Hilton."

Barbara got out a map.

"The Flake Hilton road leads to Dofton," she mused.

He read her thought. Several roads criss-crossed beyond Dofton, so no one would know where she was going if she took a different route each time to visit Jonathan.

Aldous said, "The same Estate Agent can sell our place here. Then we can rely on him keeping quiet about Mountfoot. We'll have to find a Moving Van firm that's free, hut I'll just keep phoning till I find one. We'll have to make sure the Mover workers don't answer any questions from neighbours here in Edendale... we'll sort out everything tomorrow."

* * *

Aldous picked up the keys to Mountfoot, and was back at Edendale at eleven o'clock.

Mountfoot was a cottage right up against a narrow back road, badly metalled. They saw no traffic.

The front door led into a short hall, with two doors to the left, one to a room for hanging wet coats and leaving umbrellas and muddy boots, the other with a washbasin and lavatory.

A door opened into the living room, about fifty feet long and thirty-five feet wide. The ceiling was timbered, with richly panelled walls, the windows in deep embrasures with wide stone ledges. The walls were about three feet thick. To their left, bookcases filled the wall. The sidewalls had five windows each, and the backwall was taken up by a wide kitchen behind a counter, with a heavy curtain over the counter, that could be drawn back. Behind the kitchen was a deep pantry, and a stairway up to the first floor.

On the floor above, a passage ran along the front of the house, with doors giving off to four bedrooms whose windows overlooked the back.

"The passage protects the bedrooms from the noise of the road," said Barbara pleased.

At the beginning of the passage, a door led to a narrow room with wash basin and lavatory, and at the far end, a large bathroom, above the small washroom downstairs at the entry.

"Well," said Aldous. "Bravo for Eric's voices. This is fantastic."

Another door led to a narrow cupboard, where they found thick, woven hessian matting rolled up, and rolled up carpets,

Barbara said, "In winter, you lay the hessian on the stone floor in the living-room and the carpets over that."

They went downstairs, and counted six storage heaters in the living-room.

Out back, they explored a wide, flagged patio, and crossed to a great stable. The front part took two cars, the back was empty, with nails on the walls.

"I can run cords from the nails to hang out the clothes, here inside, when it rains."

Eric was staring at the nails and had turned white. Aldous looked and felt his blood freeze. Jocelyn looked at them, and nodded, and Aldous put his finger to his lips.

While Barbara walked around, followed by Helen, the three went outside.

"My God," said Aldous.

"How horrible," whispered Jocelyn.

"He slipped off a bale of hay," said Eric.

An eighteen-year-old had slipped off the top of hales of hay, and dragged his neck over one of the nails, ripping open the jugular artery or jugular vein.

His father had desperately pressed a cloth to his son's neck.

"Don't let me die, dad," pleaded the young man.

"You're all right, Johnny," said his father. "I'll look after you. It's all right, hear."

And the life ebbed out of him, and consciousness faded from him, and the father went almost mad. In their minds, in concert, they followed the father over the next three years, till he could come to terms with it...

The three looked at each other, sickened.

"Not a word," said Aldous.

"Not a word," promised Jocelyn.

Eric choked, "I would have known it was going to happen and not got up there –"

"He didn't know," said Aldous.

* * *

Barbara came out and said worriedly, "Those thick stone walls will make the place an ice-box in winter."

"The Estate Agent said they were hollow. Very big air cavities."

"And that stone floor. Suppose there is damp."

"The place has got a dry-course, and there's a cellar running the entire length. The Council made them brick up the entry."

"What Council was that?"

"Appleby. That's where you'd have your supermarket and shops. It's only a few minutes."

13

"Why should they brick up the cellar?"

"Not a clue. Isn't it curious?" Aldous added, "We can put heavy drapes over the windows for winter."

They went through the house, locked up, and stood on the roadside.

The road ran down to Flake Hilton, and beyond the lower slopes of the Pennines reared high into the sky. In front of them lay a wood; they crossed the road and walked down looking for a path into the trees.

They found a track, followed it, and it led to an old, mossy cart track. The trees were close, with heavy foliage, a riot of every hue of green, and the canopy closed out the sky. After a quarter of a mile, the cart track came to a wooden gate, but when Aldous touched it, the cross beam crumbled under his fingers. The wood was drenched, covered in fine moss, and rotted to wet cardboard. The green-covered fence on each side had collapsed, so they stepped around the gate, and followed the wide track.

A fine, narrow path led off on one side, and they picked their way along it, over mossy rocks, muddy ground and boles of trees. It twisted this way and that, and suddenly they found themselves in a long, wide open field completely surrounded by the green of dense trees.

The children shrieked in excitement.

"We can play here and nobody will ever find us," cried Helen.

Barbara marvelled, "They kept cattle here and the Border raiders never found them."

"They might have seen the place from the slopes of the Pennines, but I bet they never climbed up."

"No," said Barbara. "This ridge probably hides it even from someone up there."

On the far side of the field, a ridge sloped up, thick with tall trees.

Eric said, "You know that Arnside Tower, hidden in the valley there in all that forest? The Border raiders never found that either. Everyone used to drive their cattle into the valley and then protect themselves inside the Tower. But this is a much better idea. I wonder where they used to live?"

"They probably built a rough wooden cottage at the edge of the field, and it's rotted away a century ago."

Jocelyn said, "With mum teaching us, we're going to be whiz kids, and we'll come here to play. No more bullies, no other kids – !"

She skipped out into the field, then began dancing and whirling. Helen raced around in circles, yelling in excitement.

Eric ran out, grabbed Jocelyn's hand, and they raced down to the far end in the brown grass.

Helen stopped still, then yelled again. "Look! A Roundhead soldier! A cow's chasing him and he's climbed up a tree!"

Everyone stopped in astonishment.

Helen burst into a little girl's giggles.

* * *

Four days later, they were living at Mountfoot.

The next morning, Aldous left at ten, drove through Appleby and down to Orton. In Orton, he found a public phone and rang Constance.

She answered on the second ring, and when she heard his voice, she said, "You bloody bastard! You said were coming back almost a week ago!"

"I did, but we had to get out of Edendale. We're in a cottage near Flake Hilton."

"And you couldn't ring!"

"It's been unalloyed madness. You must understand. Jocelyn told her teacher that two Roundhead soldiers were standing on each side of her, with bloodstained pikes, looking at her."

"Goodness! What happened?"

"Constance, she scared the teacher out of her skin. The teachers now are teaching their classes giving surreptitious glances to their right and to their left. Barbara is going to teach the children at home. Eric was being bullied at school, and a couple of the bullies lived in Edendale. Barbara found herself a posh lover, and the village soon knew."

"Are you coming now to see me?" she demanded with a rising voice.

"Of course I am. I'm in Orton."

He drove another few miles and reached the high, wrought, verdigis gates. He got out and rang, and they swung open.

He drove up the long drive, around to the back of the house, and parked on the wide gravel drive.

Constance stood in the doorway.

"We've got the place to ourselves. No cleaning women this morning." She said it, unsmiling.

Constance was twenty-eight, with creamy skin, a beautiful, deceptively innocent face, rich auburn hair, and was dressed simply in an enormously expensive twin-set of pale grey.

He took her in his arms, smelling her fragrance, and begged, "Please do forgive me, but I've been driven crazy."

"Not one brief phone call," she pouted.

"Darling, you're the only woman in the whole world, but I had such impossible headaches..."

She led him inside, and he pulled her to him again, seeking her small, firm breasts. She kissed him, with her tongue in his mouth, then pulled him through a wide foyer to the staircase.

"How is my boy?" he asked.

"He's still hearing voices and seeing these people no one else can, so I

15

do as you told me. I tell him it's all right because he's a special person, but that he mustn't tell anyone except me. Certainly not his father."

She laughed awkwardly. "Well, you're his father, but he thinks my husband is."

Her husband was an architect, and Constance had three children by him, apart from her son, Claude, by Aldous.

"I hardly ever see that husband of mine now. He's got all those girl friends down in London, he hardly comes up any more. Who are his girl friends?" She stopped outside the bedroom door and. stared at him expectantly.

Aldous concentrated.

"Two girls, one of eighteen and the other nineteen."

"Bastard," she said. "Well, at twenty-eight, I'm over the hill."

"Not for me you're not."

They went inside and began undressing. "What has he got to offer them, for God's sake?" Aldous concentrated, undoing his buttons.

"Almost every night he takes them to restaurants and night clubs. They give him group sex."

"In a night club, one or the other is going to get picked up by someone younger!" she protested.

"He offers them too much."

They were naked, and tumbled on the bed. He ran his hands over her breasts, still firm after four children, over her slim belly with the silky skin and fine layer of chubbiness, then slid his hand between her legs. She began to groan, and he entered her, his hands seeking her slim buttocks. She groaned and cried aloud and as the long minutes passed, she grew wilder and wilder. When finally he finished, she collapsed, satiated and exhausted.

Later, she said, "I want to have one more child, but you keep telling me he won't be born psychic. When can we do it and he will he psychic?"

Aldous concentrated, then smiled slowly.

"Today," he said.

"Today!" she squealed, and twisted off the bed. "Let me get rid of this pessary cap and wash away the jelly."

She came back and threw herself at him, and he thrust into her. He finished quickly, pouring himself into her, then lay quietly, stroking her soft belly which soon would swell and grow. And as he stroked it and thought of it swelling, he grew hard again, and went into her anew.

* * *

That evening, after supper, they sat in the armchairs and on the sofa, the wall lamps reflecting the dark gloss of the panelling, and picking out the beams in the ceiling.

Helen pouted, "Mummy has locked off the television again. Why can't we watch it?"

Aldous said, "You'll see documentary videos if they have to do with your lessons. You don't watch the telly, you read."

Jocelyn said eagerly, "We're reading aloud THE CLOISTER AND THE HEARTH. We can have some reading now, please, can we?"

Aldous looked at Barbara. "That's Charles Reid, isn't it?"

Eric demanded of his father, "Spell 'Reade'."

"R - e - i - d."

Eric triumphantly corrected him.

Aldous said, "That's Gerard somebody in the fourteen hundreds who has to flee England and goes to Germany, Holland, Italy, I don't know where else?"

Jocelyn said, "Daddy's the cleverest man in the whole world. Can I go first?"

She read:

> Gerard was getting very impatient, when at last the door
> opened. But it was not Denys. Entered softly an imposing
> figure; an old gentleman in a long sober gown trimmed
> with rich fur, cherry coloured hose, and pointed shoes.

Helen interrupted. "Daddy, why don't you ever dress cherry coloured and put on pointed shoes?"

"Sssh," said Jocelyn, annoyed. "Listen to me."

> – with a sword by his side in a morocco scabbard, a
> ruff round his neck not only starched severely, but
> treacherously stiffened in furrows by rebatoes, or a
> little hidden framework of wood;

"What's a ruff?" demanded Helen.

Barbara got up and fetched the English Duden, a pictorial dictionary, and showed her the picture.

Jocelyn gave an exasperated sigh. She went on:

> and on his head a four-cornered cap with a fur border; on
> his chin and bosom a majestic white beard.

Helen cried, "Daddy, you must grow a majestic white beard," and Aldous gave her a mock ferocious scowl that made her giggle.

17

Gerard was in no doubt as to the vocation of his visitor, for, the sword excepted, this was familiar to him as the full dress of a physician. Moreover, a boy followed at his heels with a basket, where phials, lint and surgical tools rather courted than shunned observation. The old gentleman came softly to the bedside, and said mildly and sotto voce, "How is't with thee, my son?"

Gerard answered gratefully that his wound gave him little pain now; hut that his throat was parched, and his head heavy.

"A wound! they told me not of that. Let me see it. Ay, ay, a good clean bite. The mastiff had sound teeth that took this out, I warrant me" and the good doctor's sympathy seemed to run off to the quadruped he had conjured, his jackal.

Barbara said, "Jocelyn, you read beautifully. Now let Eric take his turn."

Jocelyn protested, "Oh, mum, let me read a bit more." Eric got up and took the book firmly from her. "That wasn't bad, but when I read everyone gets bated breath, a truth known to all." He read out:

"This must he cauterised forthwith –"

"I don't understand corterized," complained Helen.

Eric explained, "You burn the wound with red hot irons, the patient screams in awful agony and the room fills up with the aroma of cooking meat."

Helen put her hands over her ears and began to cry. Aldous picked her up, hugged her and said, pulling her hand away, "Eric's teasing you. It means to kill all the germs with something hot."

"...cauterised forthwith, or we shall have you starting back from water –"

Aldous said to Helen, "If you get rabies from a dog's bite, you get convulsions if you touch water."

"...and turning somersaults in bed under our hands. 'Tis a year for raving curs, and one hath done your business; but we will baffle him yet. Urchin, go heat your iron."

"No!" screamed Helen.

"It's all right," said Eric. You'll see, now." He read:

18

"But, sir," edged in Gerard, "twas no dog, but a bear."

Aldous lay back, looking at the glow of the lights on the dark panelling.

"A bear! Young man," remonstrated the senior severely, "think what you say; 'tis ill jesting with the man of art who brings his gray hairs and long study to heal you. A bear, quotha! Had you dissected as many bears as I, or the tithe, and drawn their teeth to keep your hand in, you would know that no bear's jaw ever made this foolish, trifling wound. I tell you 'twas a dog, and, since you put me to it, I even deny that it was a dog of magnitude, but neither more nor less than one of these little furious curs that are so rife, and run devious, biting each manly leg, and laying its wearer low, but for me and my learned brethren, who still stay the mischief with knife and cautery."

Aldous bestirred himself. "Now me!" he announced.
"But father, it's the best part now!" cried Eric.
"No, my turn," grinned Aldous, reaching for the book.

"Alas, sir! when said I 'twas a bear's jaw; I said, 'A bear': it was his paw, now."
"And why didst not tell me that at once?"
"Because you kept telling me instead."
"Never conceal aught from your leech, young man," continued the senior, who was a good talker, but one of the worst listeners in Europe. "Well, it is an ill business. All the horny excrescences of animals, to wit, claws of tigers, panthers, badgers, cats, bears and children are imbued with direst poison..."

Helen jumped up. "I am not poisonous, and I don't have exkressances –"
"Of course you do," said Jocelyn scornfully.
"What exkressances?" demanded Helen.
"Your fingernails, silly."
"Mummy, tell her that my fingernails aren't poisonous," wept Helen.
Aldous handed the book to Barbara, and picked up Helen. He kissed her fingernails and looked at the others.
"Indeed, they are lovely fingernails, and not poisonous. Barbara, your turn to read."

19

In his London flat, the bell rang and Aldous opened the door to a lady in her mid-forties. He led her in and sat her down. She was overweight – a little – and dressed in dark clothes that hung on her badly. Her face was drawn with lines, yet immature, hopeful, for her years.

She twisted her hands, then put them in her lap, crossed her ankles tightly, and leant forward.

"I don't know where to begin –" She hesitated.

"I think it's about your son," he encouraged her.

She looked astonished.

"Yes," she admitted, looking down at the floor. "I had my baby boy twenty-one years ago, and when he was two, my husband left me. My husband was a bit rough, I had made a mistake, so it was probably the best thing. But I met this other man, he was a salesman in a big store, a good talker, and more gentle, but he was a widower, and had three children, about ten years old. So he demanded..."

Her voice caught on a sob.

"That you give up your boy for adoption," Aldous helped her. He thought, when a pride of lions loses its male lion, and another male finds the pride, the second male kills all the cubs, so only his own cubs will survive.

"We were together for seventeen years, and now he has left me. I reared his children, but they hardly ever see me." She sobbed. "I gave them all the love and care I had..."

"Now you have someone else," Aldous prompted.

"He's fifty-one, with grown-up children who care for him. He separated from his wife some years ago."

"You want to find your son?" Aldous said, and the woman nodded eagerly, her eyes searching his face.

"Let me concentrate..." He sat in silence.

"He is in Vancouver. He has studied to be a mechanic, a car mechanic he is now, a sort of apprentice. The people who adopted him were... were Clements –"

21

"That's right," she said. "I've just found that out, under the new law."

"They went to Canada, many years ago. His first name is still Bill. Go to the Canadian Embassy, and ask instructions how to proceed. Take his birth certificate with you. You will find him shortly and you will write him a letter. He will accept your going to Vancouver."

Her face trembled. She opened her purse and handed him the money.

* * *

After she left, he paced the room.

Life ambushes you.

A car crash can leave you paraplegic.

Here, an outsider, a man, had broken her life.

Also, she had given way to her weakness, her dependency, to take a catastrophic decision, give her boy for adoption.

And – as always – she hadn't seen the future. She had fumbled blindly.

The human brain was aggressive, its desires reached the temperatures of melting steel... but it could not see the future.

So the brain was a high-powered car, driven with the accelerator to the floor, the driver blindfolded.

He stood at the window, feeling ill.

* * *

The bell rang.

He knew the couple had rung from Reading. He was heavily built, a rugged, alert face – Aldous probed gently – and was fifty-one. His wife was – was – forty-eight. She had distinguished features, imperious eyes and mouth. He sat them down, and the husband folded his hands over his tummy, while she sat up straight, looking at him directly, steepling her hands in her lap.

He coughed nervously, but she spoke with distinct enunciation.

"We have been married five years, and very happily. But my husband had been married before, and had three children, fourteen, ten and five. They live with their mother in Liverpool. My husband is a maintenance engineer, but on leaving Liverpool, he has found work in Reading doing the same work. However, most of his salary goes in payments to that woman..."

Her voice hesitated, and she recovered control.

"The money will be for the children," suggested Aldous mildly.

"And for the mother," grated the wife. "She doesn't work but stays at home all day. They still live in Liverpool. My husband makes a visit every few months to see the children, but now he has found that the mother is turning

22

the eldest, a girl, and the second, a boy, against him, brainwashing them, and telling them that their father has abandoned them."

The husband moved uncomfortably in his seat, clasping and unclasping big hands, looking worriedly at Aldous. The wife stared at him firmly.

"This is happening while my husband is paying a small fortune to keep them. So, what will happen?"

Aldous said, "If things continue as now, the children will become uncontrollable and grow into dropouts, then into unemployable young adults."

The husband's face whitened, and the wife pressed her lips together in anger at Aldous.

Unperturbed, Aldous went on, "But you have another card to play."

"What?" snapped the wife, with antagonism.

"The house in Liverpool belongs to your husband."

"That's right," said the man, astonished.

Aldous addressed himself to the lady. "You enjoy considerable resources. You could buy a house in Reading, at some distance from yourselves naturally, and offer it to the mother. That she bring her children to Reading to be educated. When she comes, your husband can sell the house in Liverpool, and recover most of the outlay."

The wife looked at him scornfully.

"The mother could never agree to *that!*"

"I can assure you that she will accept it, after a couple of weeks of thinking it over."

"I don't want to be rude, but I am sorry, I find this impossible to believe."

"I assure you that is exactly what will happen. Exactly. Never doubt it. I can see it quite clearly."

"And what do you believe we gain by this?" snapped the wife.

"Your husband will see his children every weekend. Then he can introduce them to you. They need a firm hand and a firm example, and someone to be after them every weekend on how their school week has gone. Your husband can speak to the teachers to hear the problems, and after he tells you, you can straighten the children out. They need a certain severity."

"They will stop seeing their father on the weekends," said the wife, uncertainly. "We'll frighten them away."

"No", said Aldous with certainty, "I can see exactly what will happen. They will welcome it, because it will give them a strong sense of security. In passing, you can also teach them table manners. You are going to be shocked by them."

They paid him £125 and departed with pleased smiles.

The man filled his summer suit. He was brisk, with a competent, lined face.

"I'm a businessman. I import tea, and the business is going okay. But I'm not married. Have my own house, close to my parents, but I'm not married."

He sucked air between his teeth.

"I'm in my late thirties, but my brother is much younger – twenty-seven. He's into drugs. God knows where he gets them, or how he pays for them. I hate to think what sort of crowd he hangs out with, where in God's name he goes to meet them.

"But my parents are worried sick over him. They keep him – he lives at home with them. He fills their thoughts. I go there, and I don't know whether they even see me, know that I exist. My parents mean everything to me – I'm not married, so I suppose I can say I need to lean on them emotionally. They're all I have. I need their love and understanding, I need to be close to them, I need their support and encouragement.

"But what do I get instead? I get that my brother has done this, has done that, what can we do for him?

"I'm at a breaking point. Where is all this going to end? What's it all coming to? If I break with my parents, will I have a nervous breakdown? What's going to happen?"

Aldous said, "Your brother will die. Your parents will depend on you completely in their old age. They love you as much, or more, than they love your brother.

"But you don't *need* them. Your brother does. They hope somehow they can save him. He's *their* child, and they want to rescue him.

"In a few weeks, you're going to meet someone who'll invite you to a Club. Accept the invitation and go. You'll find it a place where people talk very freely. They're all well-to-do, but they talk very freely. You'll be able to talk out your problems, and get another slant on everything from the others.

"Your parents will be absolutely dependent on you. They're in dire straits, and need all the patience and support you can afford them.

"The death of your brother will devastate them, and they will have only you to lean on."

The businessman nodded dumbly, pulled out his walled, and paid.

The banknotes were not marked.

She was a fretful housewife of about thirty, with weary lines to her face, dowdily dressed.

She sat and stared at him; and looked reassured.

"I have two children, and I'm divorced. I was a victim of domestic violence, they call it, which means I got bashed and beaten up. The police came and arrested him, and we were taken to a Centre that looked after the children, while I got medical attention, and counselling. Then they gave me psychotherapy. The psychiatrist –" she stumbled over the word – "said that just as there are reborn Christians, there are reborn victims, just waiting again and again for someone to come and hit us. He said that I see invisible signals that other people don't see, so I'm attracted to men who are going to harm me."

She paused, with tears welling to her eyes, then went on.

"I've met this man, who I am growing very fond of, but I don't trust my judgement. Is he going to be good for me?"

Aldous held up his hand, and was silent almost five minutes.

He said, "This man is a psychopath. Normally, we can't distinguish a psychopath from ordinary people until they commit some awful action or another. You understand me?"

"Oh, I understand you. The psychiatrist said my husband was a psychopath. Now you are telling me I have been attracted to another one?"

Aldous nodded.

He said, "Attend your church regularly. Attend the midweek functions too. You will meet a freckled man who will propose marriage. Accept him. You will have a long, uneventful marriage. You will not be in love with him, but he will be in love with you. He will not attract you, for reasons the psychiatrist has already warned you about.

"But you will marry him."

He looked at her soberly, but she didn't speak.

She nodded dumbly, and paid him.

The banknotes were not marked. The detectives outside were doing nothing yet.

* * *

Aldous sat in the armchair with a small whisky, deeply depressed.

Life was unabated suffering, and there was no antidote.

Alcohol, drugs, pleasures, psychiatrists – this world had no healing, no specific.

25

He had to catch the afternoon plane to Toronto. He checked his brief case, looked around the flat carefully, then carried his suitcase to inside the front door, and rang for a taxi.

When Aldous landed in Toronto, he went to his small flat in Carlton St with a view of Allan Gardens. He had left London about midday, and it was after one o'clock in Toronto. He rang neither Claude nor Susan, but showered and slept for half an hour.

At three o'clock, he went to the Investment Company in Bay Street. He strode in, nodding at Marjorie, the receptionist, and walked through the passageway between the glass partitions. People working at screens saw him and nodded. He came into a wide, carpeted reception space, smiled at his brother's secretary, knocked on Claude's frosted glass door, opened it a little and poked his head in.

Claude was alone, and looked up from his desk.

"Good lord, but it's Aldous!"

They stood there, grinning at each other.

"Where have you popped up from?"

"Just flown in from London. Doing a lot of consultations. I'm worn out."

"You do-gooder! Why don't you work on the market, instead of saving people's souls?" -

"Claude, I can't 'see' anything that benefits me myself," he lied. "If all we psychics got to work on the markets, the Stock Exchanges would all have to close." He looked regretfully at his brother.

Claude said, "We've just done the half-yearly audit, and we're ahead about two million Canadian."

"That's all right for a small family business, charging the lowest commissions on the market."

"Our commissions certainly fetch them," said Claude. "Do you want to come for dinner tonight? Mary would love to see you after so long."

"Well, you know how it is... I've got a sort of girl friend I haven't seen for weeks, and she wants to take her holidays up at Pickle Creek."

"I've been married so long, but I faintly remember 'how it is'. Want to go over the figures?"

"Not this afternoon. Anything new?"

27

The Canadian in Claude launched happily into business.

"We've hired ourselves a Risk Manager."

"Ah," said Aldous. "Let's sit down. Please explain. Sounds most interesting. Where's he from?"

"From New York. He's just gotten married, and his wife's from Toronto. She wants to live in Canada, and preferably in Toronto, and it so happened we were looking. It works like this."

Claude was a big man, like his brother, with a moon face, receding hairline, huge hands that moved quickly, his expression set into permanent lines of concentration. His forehead was smooth; he never looked worried.

He and Mary had four children, the eldest sixteen.

Claude said, "Our new Risk Manager is in charge of measuring and identifying the different financial risks of the company."

"Bravo," laughed Aldous. "Big order."

"So, he analyses interest rates. If we have a position in interest rates and the rates fall, then our clients lose and get pissed off at us. Then, of course, he analyses Stock Market risks, and while no one can predict with surety which way the market will go – not even yourself," he added, looking at Aldous dubiously, "it's surprising how he can quantify the risk within mathematical parameters. Next, we come to credit risks. What I mean are the purchase orders we accept without prior deposit of capital from the client.

"But he goes even further than that. He also calculates legal risks – you know, avoiding loopholes in the wording of our contracts with clients.

"So his job is to handle our systematic risks. We gotta diversify between say interest rates and market positions. What he's got is this computer software – it's a program called VAR, VALUE AT RISK, so that's really useful. At this moment in time, we've got about fifteen percent of our capital in stable trading portfolios, and the other eighty-five percent in reserve, invested in buildings, government debt – what have you. But we can change that. We can put two-thirds into short term Treasury Bills and we've got liquidity, so we can lend to clients for their investments, which gives us a margin of 2.75% over and above what the Treasury Bills would have given us."

Aldous said, "I'm going to have to leave you now. I've just got in and I wanted to have a bit of a holiday... that's what all this of Pickle Creek is about. Ten days canoeing up Lake St. Matthew, go on to Bluestone Lake, Bamoki – I don't suppose we'll get as far as Dog Lake. The girlfriend's got some sort of gym apparatus she's had rigged up, that imitates the action of paddling, so she's probably got muscles all over."

Claude exploded into laughter.

"So you get to caress all those muscles. Wow!"

"Well, I gotta put in some calls. I'll go to my little corner, and we'll be in touch. Okay?"

"Take care," said Claude, already going back to his table.

Aldous had his own little cubicle, in woodwork instead of frosted glass. It was small, soundproof, and it had the only phone in the office with a direct, outside line that didn't go through the switchboard.

He rang her at home, and she answered on the second ring.

"Susan? My love. Guess who?"

"You bastard! I thought you were gonna stand me up."

"I've just got into Toronto. How am I going to stand you up? I've got the plane booked, and an ATV reserved at Pickle Creek."

"I'm amazed," she snapped.

"Susan, although I'm travelling, I'm thinking about you all the time."

"Like hell – all those other women."

"Susan, there aren't any other women. I'm too busy, and thinking about you, I've got no time to worry about anyone else."

"Bloody liar."

"Susan, I've been dreaming about you morning and night, and when at last I can actually hear your voice, you treat me like this. After these weeks of dreaming of this moment."

"Well," she said mollified, "You've got a terrific line this afternoon."

"Susan, my darling, when your Lesbo friends say that they love you, I bet you believe them. But you don't me."

"My lesbian loves are sensitive, loving people, while you men are big brutes."

"And do we fly out tomorrow morning, or don't we?"

"We do."

"I'm all packed."

* * *

Aldous walked back to his flat. It was muggy, and. he sought the shade of the trees. Toronto – the City of Trees. A slight breeze carried away some of the car fumes, and he kept as far from the roadway as he could.

He ought to have planned free time to go to dinner with Claude and Mary, but it would wait. They didn't know about Barbara in England, and the three children, although his children did know about their uncles. Barbara had wanted to meet them, and he warned her that his sisters-in-law were very old-fashioned and uptight, and when they knew they had not married, they could make life hell for her. He had looked after her very well in his Will – she didn't know she would die long before he did – and that if his brothers and their wives knew about that, they would never give him rest.

"My God, just leave it alone," she begged. "So long as the Will is there."

29

As the Solicitor they both used held the document, and. she had read it, she knew where it was and what it said.

Maj-Britt had talked about his brothers too, and he told her the same story. He had another Will made out to her and her children, and one day she would inherit, although even more money than this Will stipulated. She had never hesitated. "Leave well alone," she told him.

His brothers knew about Anna in Torre Real, and thought she was married to him. Anna's father had a summer house very close to his Spanish office, run by his brother, Phil, and Anna's father was a client. Phil's wife, June, often got together with Anna when Anna went down to her father's place to spend the summer, and how those two women must gossip, one Spanish, the other English living in Spain.

* * *

He got home sweating, and hung up his suit, put away his tie, and put his underwear and shirt in the washing machine. When the Phillipine cleaning woman came, she would put everything away.

He put on shorts, a light linen shirt with sandals and packed his backpack with care, took the clothes out of the machine, and hung them up.

Susan lived in Ponytail St., with a view of Forest Park.

Her rang her again.

"How goes the job?"

Susan was a designer.

"One client's pretty profitable, but the General Manager is sexually harassing me. I'd love to take him to court and rip him off for a really solid settlement, but then I'd never find work again in Canada. And a lady Manager is leaning on me too. She's a butch, a dike, whatever's the word *you* use, and I can't stand that."

Susan took the 'male' role with her lesbian loves.

"I've got a wonderful new girl friend. Stephanie. She's so submissive and insecure and so much in love with me. She wants to come tonight, as it's my last night..."

"And make me jealous?" chuckled Aldous. "Doesn't she know that what I feel for you is admiration, and that for your remarkable canoeing skills?"

"You bastard," pouted Susan.

Susan said, "I've bought a couple of screens I set up in the back garden and I've been sunbathing. I've got my tan all over."

"Remember my office in Spain at Torre Real? I've been on the beach, thinking about our trip and getting this colour."

"And nary a glance at all the tits around you?"

"I am a one-girl man."

They flew on a regular flight to Thunder Bay, then caught a ten-seater feeder plane to Pickle Creek. After they landed, and collected their packs and duffle bags, a tall, hefty, bearded man, wearing a tartan shirt, came over and said, "Mr. Windsor? Got your ATV here," and handed Aldous the keys. He helped Susan with her duffle bag over to the four-wheel drive, and drove them into town. "We'll go to the office to sign all the papers, and then you can be off."

"You're new," said Aldous. "How's Mr. Scott?"

"Well, I bought him out. He left. You've been this aways before?"

"Got a cabin down on St. Matthew lake."

"Go on! So we'll be seeing you on and off quite a bit. You told me two weeks on the phone, so you're stopping there?"

"Going canoeing. I've got a lean-to lock-up at the back of the cabin, so I'll leave your vehicle in there."

"Been coming up here long?"

"Years. Know several people here. So if we drown without a trace –"

"You bastard," grimaced Susan, then laughed. "He's got this great sense of humour," she said to their driver.

The bearded man was grinning.

"– the cabin's registered in town," Aldous finished.

* * *

They signed the papers, shopped for food, cleaning materials and toiletries, and drove 40 km down to the cabin. They left the asphalt road, and turned along a logging road that ended in a wide clearing, where they picked up a narrow dirt track that led to the cabin close to the water's edge.

The cabin was rectangular, built of logs, and raw logs formed the inside walls. Eight bunks lined the four walls. Aldous opened the four windows, released the heavy shutters and pushed them up and secured them.

A long table ran down the centre, with benches, and they dumped their gear on it. Beside it stood a round-bellied iron stove, the iron chimney crossing the room to the roof on the far side. Four rocking chairs with cushions were pushed beside a bunk. Under the bottom bunk on the back wall lay a 16-foot canoe.

They pulled out waterproof plastic bags, and tied their packs and duffle bags inside. They carried the canoe over the stony beach, and laid it rocking in the water, while they lashed in the bags.

Closing up the cabin, they slid out into the waters of the lake, and paddled close inshore.

It was 4.05 pm.

They followed the shore for thirty minutes, and then the land twisted sharply away from then. They headed into the open lake to the next headland, about two miles away, and drove cleanly through the water.

"We're in fine fettle for starters," said Aldous. "Let's see if we can keep it up. For a wee feminine wisp of crayture, you're plying a mean paddle."

"That's enough from you, you hairy chauvinist. I hope your ageing bones don't begin to creak."

"Youth always will envy the wisdom that comes only with the years."

They closed with the headland, and beyond it, the shore took a shallow curve away from them. Herons circled and wove close by the beach. They cut straight across and came up to the shore again, the water littered with outcrops of rocks, shingled beach lying behind.

"Let's have a look at that beach," said Aldous. "Stop paddling."

He wove gently among the rocks, and the duro-aluminium hull scraped on the grey and yellow-brown stones.

"We could've slept tonight at the cabin," grumbled Susan, stepping ashore, and pulling on the gunwale to line the canoe up with the edge of the water.

Aldous stepped ashore, and while Susan held the canoe, he walked into the trees. Fallen trees lay everywhere, propped against standing trees or sprawling on the ground. His feet trod on uneven earth and boulders, some boulders half covered with earth and vegetation. Broad-leafed plants grew knee-high, brushing and catching his legs. Blackflies, yellow jackets and other insects buzzed, whined and circled, held away by his insect gel. He trod and lurched among black spruce, white spruce, jacket pine and balsam fir. He came on no clearings, and went back to the canoe.

"Let's go up further. This place's no good."

He got in the back, Susan in the front, and she pushed away with the handle of her paddle. The canoe floated free, and Aldous paddled slowly through the rocks to open water.

They followed up the shore a couple of miles, and saw a flat headland. They could see across it to the lake on the other side. Aldous steered to it, and then he paddled very slowly, by himself, till they inched into a beach of gravel and smooth stones. Susan stepped ashore, and pulled the canoe around, and Aldous got out.

He walked through the broad-leafed, knee high plants, on flat, grassy earth. Three or four grey trunks leaned askew on living trees – plenty of firewood.

"It's flat, but no protection against the wind."

It had gone five o'clock, and he looked up at the cloudless sky. A slow breeze stirred the poplar and birch branches, and the insects were not insistent here.

"Let's unload. What do you think?" He held the canoe while she walked around.

"Nice spot. Very nice. Not too rocky."

"Well, as you'll he lying underneath me," he said complacently. "Pneumatic bliss, pneumatic comfort..."

"Don't you count on that," she said, pulling at the lashings.

They unloaded, pulled up the canoe, and put up the beehive tent.

Aldous cut branches from the dead trees, and got a fire going. He built a tripod with green wood; and Susan boiled water, hanging the pot from the tripod, while Aldous set out the canvas chairs, and blew up the air-mattress. The smoke was aromatic.

After eating, and washing the dishes, they sat watching the light die in the sky, and hillsides on the far side of the lake darken.

Night would not fall until very late.

* * *

Their love-making was wild. Susan knew no inhibition. Afterwards, Aldous lay in exhaustion. Then they got up, stood with their feet in the chilling water, and washed. They sat and drank fruit juice, and ate chocolate. "I'm sure that was an improvement on Stephanie," remarked Aldous.

"You men know nothing about making love. You dive in, thinking only about your own pleasure and impregnating us. We're just receptacles for your semen. Another woman is exquisitely sensitive to you when she makes love. She knows and explores every nuance, every thread of feeling and pleasure that pierces you."

"Wow!" said Aldous. "She rides right along on your orgasm. That's what I call vicarious. Would you like another vicarious ride on one of my orgasms?"

"Well, now," Susan said coquettishly. "Well – that's an idea, but I don't think you've got it in you."

Aldous grinned ruefully. "I guess you're right. I might be able to manage just half the job."

"Ah," said Susan. "The first half, or the second?"

"The first half, I guess."

34

"No way. I'm only interested in the second part of this business."

* * *

The heat went out of the day. They lay on their sleeping bags, with light blankets over them. During the night, they woke up chilled, and got inside their bags.

Next morning, they breakfasted on bacon and sausages, pancakes and maple syrup, followed by cups of coffee with powdered milk.

At ten, they slid the canoe into the lake. The morning was cloudless, the sun bright on the water, changing it to blue. Then a breeze sprang up, and white clouds sped across the sky, widely spaced. A faint ruffle broke up the water of the lake into thousands of glints and sparkles – they had to put on their polaroid glasses, although the sun was to their side. Lake St Matthew needed about 150 km of paddling, before they got to the river leading to Bluestone lake, and Aldous reckoned they'd need four days to get to the top of it. They were not in any sort of training.

They passed a headland and cut straight across the lake, more than a mile out. A bald-headed eagle soared over the ridge, and settled on a majestic bluff. The shore slowly came towards them, the trees standing like grim spearmen, dark green and watchful. The trees mounted the slopes, and shields of grey rocks broke into their ranks. Miles along, short escarpments of rock broke into the trees, and then the spearmen regrouped, sharp points to the sky.

They followed the shore for some miles, and suddenly a deep unease possessed Aldous. He did not stop paddling, but looked carefully at the sky. A warm summer sky. His premonition grew. He glanced around the waters of the lake, looking for a swimming bear. He stared at the treeline, his mind violently probing beyond it. He saw a caribou come out of the water and stampede into the trees.

Nothing.

He said urgently, "Susan, hold it a sec."

He leant forward, untied the neck of the plastic sack in front of him, and eased out his rifle. He laid it down beside the sack, and tied up the neck of the bag again.

He lifted up the rifle and chambered a round into the breech, then released the magazine, checked it and snapped it on again.

He pushed the rifle under a lashing, the rifle pointing out into the lake, then stared around him, probing... probing...

His foreboding grew, gathered –

"Let's get ashore, fast," he said.

They both paddled hard, and Susan called, "But what is it?"

"Damned if I know. I can't get it, I can't!"

Susan cried, "Keep at it! Keep trying!"

Was a meteorite coming in, invisible, to hit the lake? An earth tremor to send a wave racing across the water? An underwater eruption? He could catch animal brains – but nothing.

They reached the shore, a muddy bank, about three feet high, with stones along the bottom. Susan jumped out, pulled around the canoe, and together they manhandled their cargo up onto the bank. Susan climbed up, and Aldous tipped up one end of the canoe to her, and they got it over the bank.

They stood staring at the lake, then at the forest behind them, then back at the lake.

Then Aldous saw it - a shining, disc-shaped, flying object coming towards them at an extraordinary speed.

"Back into the trees," he said. "There's some sort of US Airforce experimental plane and I don't think anyone's supposed to see it. If they see observers, we might be in serious trouble."

It came over the lake, slowed suddenly, defying every law of gravity and inertia. It settled down to ten feet above the water, and slowly drifted over to them.

They stared in horror.

Aldous heard a telepathic voice in his head, "Don't be alarmed, old chap. Take it easy."

He gaped, and 'sent', "Right you are."

He turned to Susan, and said, "It's all right. It looks pretty crazy, but it's really okay."

He squeezed tight his bowels and bladder.

The disc emitted no sound. It came very slowly up to the bank.

It was about 140 feet across.

A telepathic message came, "This probably looks like nothing you've ever seen, hut we call it a sort of scooter, just for running around in."

"It's a scooter," said Aldous to Susan, to reassure her, and she gave him an unbelieving look, on the edge of hysteria.

36

A panel slid back on the upper side, and a long platform extended to where they stood.

A sort of spider, more than six feet across, with four legs and four arms, each ending in six fingers and a thick neck holding a spherical head with two eyes and. a wide mouth, strode out quickly.

Beside him, Susan began screaming and shrieking uncontrollably, and as her knees gave way, Aldous got a telepathic message, "Grab her, she can hit her head.."

Aldous caught her, and lowered her to the ground.

He stared at the creature.

The skin was tough, brownish green, with short hairs or bristles.

Aldous began breathing very fast and felt himself grow dizzy.

The creature 'sent', "You're hyperventilating. Get a grip on yourself."

Aldous breathed slowly and deeply.

The creature sent, "I see you find me very ugly. But if you could see yourself. Balancing on two spindly legs. How do you stay upright?"

"We've got automatic brain circuits. Only when our balance is threatened, do we think about it consciously."

"Evolution has played a joke on you. And those tiny feet – I suppose they help?"

Aldous babbled, "Our feet have 26 bones, 19 muscles, well over a hundred ligaments and nerve endings by the thousands."

"Sounds pretty messy."

Aldous blathered, "There are a quarter of a million sweat glands on each foot. We do about 20,000 steps a day normally."

The creature sent, "My name is Zuxkirw, and I'm from the planet XHEMPTUW. That is thirty light years from here. Seventy years ago, we began receiving electronic signals from you, and finally we localised your planet. We studied the signals for forty years, and finally deciphered your speech. At first it sounded like one long sound! My planet is ruled by the Supreme Committee, and over some 200 light years, there are eight more planets. The nine planets are ruled by the Grand Council, and it is the Grand Council which has sent me, to find out about you, and finally to advance your science by 3,000 years in the first instance. I came here on a yacht, which came in over Hudson Bay. I scanned all the north of this continent, and could only find you. You humans aren't psychic, is that it? Are you an exception, is that it?"

"Yes, I'm an exception. But if you want to find out about the human race, I'm no good to you. You should land on the White House lawn."

"In your electronic broadcasts – radio and television – we have formed an unflattering picture of your leaders. I wish to stay with you, if I may."

"We're going to attract some attention."

"Not to worry. You seem well informed. All that about the feet. You could have knocked me over with a feather."

"Indeed," said Aldous dubiously.

"Would you like to come and see my yacht?"

"I don't know about Susan – my God!" he had forgotten her, and she was unconscious on the ground. He knelt.

"Not to worry. It was I who put her to sleep. I don't think her hysteria was good for her."

Four metallic robots flew out of the disc, picked her up and floated her in through the opening.

Aldous sent "Would you give me a moment. I must attend to a call of nature. Serious emergencies can affect our bowels."

He went over behind the trees. He came back, lowered himself down the bank to the lake, and washed his hands.

"An involved ritual," the Xhemptuwen sent.

"Germs," sent Aldous.

"Ah, very dangerous. We brought them under control hundreds of thousands of years ago."

Aldous followed him inside. They walked into a domed hall, a pale, glowing green, with doors leading off. Zuxkirw stood at a curved console and pressed buttons. Inside, Aldous heard a hum, but had no sensation of movement. He sat on a bench, which held him.

Aldous sent, "There are military satellites all over the sky. You're under surveillance. They'll probably send military jets."

Zuxkirw sent, "They can't see us. We create a shimmer over our surfaces."

"You seem to defy gravity. Coming in, you braked so hard a human would have been crushed to pulp."

"Defying the gravity! Not even after half a million years. We annul what we call the Zero Point Field, and our mass, what you call the Higgs Particle. We make ourselves massless and so don't respond to gravitons."

"How can you breathe our atmosphere?"

"We don't breathe. What do you breathe for? To be able to speak? From your electronic emissions, we have gathered that you communicate by sounds and by sight – by sight, I mean reading and writing."

"That's right."

"And no telepathic contact? That's appalling."

"We breathe because we use the oxygen to supplement our energy supply, especially with increased effort, like running."

"Energy from air! You have to be joking. What a meagre source!"

"That's the way we do it."

"Evolution has played another joke on you. I can lift about two tons and can run at about sixty miles an hour – although God knows, what for! Why I'd ever do that? Three hundred thousand years ago, we lived on another planet – a beautiful place like yours – but it was devastated by asteroid and comet bombardment. We went to a hot, rocky planet, which was completely safe, and had to grow our food artificially. So we made it more and more energetic, and genetically adapted our bodies to consume this energetic nourishment. Are you humans working on this?"

"No, we can't increase our energetic intake unless we go to the North Pole, and try to cross it on foot. We eat more, we get fat."

"The energy in our food comes from our sun. Isn't it the same here? Yet, we see atrocious scenes in your TV broadcasts. We see carnivorous animals attacking, killing and eating herbivorous ones."

"The plants absorb sunlight. Animals eat the plants for about eight or ten hours a day. After months or years, their bodies represent a store of converted sunlight. A lion eats a gnu, and has enough for a week. He eats only two or three hours a week."

"What a barbaric system! There is nothing like that in our confederation of planets."

Zuxkirw touched a button, and a large panel came alive, showing a space ship below. He sent, "That's my yacht. It's three km across. You can see it because we are penetrating the protective screen. Look!"

He touched another button, and all Aldous saw was dully rippling light waves.

Zuxkirw sent, "It was under water, in Hudson Bay. Now it's come up, to let us in."

On the screen, he saw them fly into a cavernous hanger.

They left the disc, and found themselves in a lofty, light green, glowing cavern. Robots bore Susan. They sat on a platform, which carried them swiftly to the far end, through an opening into a long, glowing corridor, which twisted and turned, and came to a deep, hollow well. They hovered in the centre, then dropped slowly through empty space, and at a deeper level, went into another corridor.

They entered a high-ceilinged, wide room, full of apparatus.

Zuxkirw sent, "I want to borrow some of your genes and some from Susan, to make a half-brother of yours, and I will occupy that brother, taking on, I think, the name of Gulliver."

He paused. "Speaking of genes, we found a planet about forty light-years from ours – about seventy light years from here. They had 'selfish genes'. The males raped the females and killed other males, who, of course, carried rival genes. We had to see whether we would ban them from going out into space, but I reported back they were millennia from space-faring. They did have metals and villages. They were so busy killing and raping, they had no time for technology."

The alien looked keenly at Aldous. "I seem to read in your mind and in your past that if you have selfish genes on this planet, your particular

39

selfish genes seem to have found an ideal spreader, in yourself."

Aldous said, shocked, "We don't have selfish genes here! I try only to make women happy, and to give them psychically-gifted children, to help them in life."

Zuxkirw beamed him the thought. "Certainly, you don't seem personally to kill men."

Aldous was outraged.

Zuxkirw sent, "You can have males who rape but don't kill, males who kill but don't rape, and those that do both. All three actions help your own selfish genes.

"How many humans have been killed in this century?"

Aldous said thoughtfully, "In wars, only about 200 million. We have some 6,000 million people on Earth."

The Xhemptuwen asked, "And individual murders?"

Aldous said, "It used to be *much* worse... in some places over historical time, about one man in two died violently."

Zuxkirw sent, "So the humans who kill in wars are not rapists – they simply eradicate rival gene carriers."

Aldous said indignantly, "We go to war for democracy... justice... peace... for the happiness of the oppressed. Our leaders have explained – spelt it out for us. To stop others from exterminating us."

"Do you indeed," came the thought of the alien. "Well, as I am going to use your replicated genes, I do hope I don't catch any selfish genes from you to disturb my equanimity."

"I haven't got a selfish gene in my body," said Aldous stoutly. "I have simply taken more responsibility than most other men to make women happy. Women *need* orgasms."

Aldous lost consciousness.

Aldous came to, invigorated, bursting with energy. He didn't know where he was. Then he remembered, he had a long holiday – a canoe trip. He opened his eyes, saw lights in the domed ceiling, pale green, glowing walls...

He swung lightly to his feet, stupefied, and then remembered. He quickly swept the room, and saw a man standing, smiling at him.

The other was a three-quarters image of himself, older, thinner, and a couple of inches shorter.

He grinned at Aldous, and said, "Gulliver at your service. Your half-brother in the flesh."

Aldous looked at him dazedly, incredulous. He finally gasped, "How long have I been out?"

"Eleven days."

Aldous stared, unable to speak. The silence grew.

He stuttered, "This is a complete adult body. How have you built this in eleven days?"

"We followed a new world line back for 48 years, mixing your genes with those of Susan. The face was largely cloned directly from yourself."

Aldous shook his head. "A world line?" he begged.

"It has been suggested here by Stephen Hawking. It is a train of events which might have happened, or could happen, or does happen. In this case, I was a person who might have happened. We went back 48 years and made it happen."

Aldous jumped back on to the table and sat, dumbly.

"Look, I know I sound pretty thick." He stopped again, then sighed.

"How do you compress 48 years into eleven days?"

"By going into the Third Dimension."

"Ask a stupid question, and get a stupid answer," he groaned. He took a deep breath. "What is the Fourth Dimension?"

"The *Third* Dimension," Gulliver corrected him, reprovingly. "In the Third Dimension, change in our Universe can be accelerated. We accelerated change – well, time, as you understand it – we accelerated time so that on

41

Earth, about four years and seven plus months passed for each day in the Third Dimension. As I say, we went back 48 years, and robots popped back into normal Earth time; that night, they entered the London Registry of Births. I was inscribed that night, and the employees were subjected to hypnotic suggestion. We also made out a Birth Certificate. When time came to go to school, we popped back to earth, and I was registered at a Primary School. The staff of the School suffered hypnotic suggestion never to see the entry, although they looked at it. Each year, I was registered as passing to the next Grade. Likewise, Grammar School, and then University. I graduated in Geology, and have the Certificates. All the time, my body was growing normally, as does that of any human, but in a very accelerated way. We got Geology textbooks, which I studied. When I turned 27, one night we popped back to earth, entered by night the Passport Office, and made out a Passport in my name, all in order. I went to Australia – my entry was registered one midnight – where I spent years prospecting in the Outback. Came to Canada, where 'I have been prospecting.' All the paperwork is in order."

Aldous sat speechlessly.

"Well, he said wearily, "And what is the Second Dimension?"

"Where you are living. This Universe."

"And the First Dimension?"

"Where you and I came from originally. Our Spirit home. What you call heaven. Do you believe in heaven?"

Aldous said tiredly, "You have come to a civilisation on its last legs. Our religions have collapsed. In the advanced countries, we believe... well, I don't know... I suppose we believe our scientists. They are our new High Priests. There are about 2,000 eminent scientists who stand above all the rest, and most of them don't believe in God. Scientists teach us that what is real is only what we can register with our senses, either directly, or indirectly with the help of instruments, or of megainstruments."

"WHAT!" exclaimed Gulliver. He paused. "Please, one minute."

He pressed a button on the watch he wore, and said:

Urgent. Gulliver reporting:

Primitive Earth science and technology is ruled by some 2,000 scientists, who teach that reality is what human senses can register directly or through instruments. Senses here register only one percent of Confederation capacity.

End.

Aldous gaped.

"I have to report back to the nine planets. I think 'urgent' is the wrong word to use. Translated, it means the message receives direct priority for transmission to the Supreme Committees of the Nine Planets, and to the Grand Council itself."

"What are you reporting?" wavered Aldous.

Then he said unsteadily, 'What are you here for?"

"I have come to report on Earth. For Earth to join the Confederation of the Nine Planets. We will advance your knowledge, your science by 3,000 years in the first instance. It will take you fifty years to assimilate what we will give you, and then we will slowly take you hundreds of thousands of years into the future in a question of centuries. The history of humanity will be divided into the period before my arrival, and the period that follows. Your lives, your medicine, your technology will be transformed beyond all imagining."

Aldous said, "But first you must check?"

"The Grand Council is very unhappy. At first, we received your electronic signals with a delay of 30 years more or less. We sent a booster robot which captures your signals, sends them into the Fourth Dimension, from whence we extract them with a delay only of hours. We don't like your leaders. The Grand Council was very upset by Hitler, Mussolini, Stalin, Roosevelt, Churchill, and now by Pinochet, that man in Belgrade, by Clinton, Blair, and Yeltsin – the list is large. They are upset by Clinton, and debated him for ten minutes."

Aldous was staggered. "Debated where?"

"On a planet about 120 light years from here. It lies towards the centre of the Confederation."

"So the message you have just sent will go through the Fourth Dimension and arrive in hours?"

Aldous waved his hand abstractedly, then ran his fingers through his hair.

He said, "You're going to bowl me over with a feather. We're running out of Dimensions here."

Gulliver said cheerfully, "The Fourth Dimension is one of speeds far greater than the speed of light. I came to earth through it."

"And why such an enormous ship?"

"It's a buffeting ride. Also, my yacht carries immense firepower – a smaller craft couldn't carry some of the systems. I don't want Clinton launching his Airforce against me and find myself defenceless."

"And the First Dimension – things move slowly there, in heaven?"

"There's no limit to speed in heaven, but one doesn't track through the First to get from one place to another in this Universe. It'd be like setting up a shoe repair stall beside St. Peter's High Altar in the Vatican."

"I don't quite see the parallel, but I get the idea," said Aldous. "So

43

you're going to push us forward 3,000 years in science? I don't see how."

Gulliver gave him a sudden, intense, concentrated look.

"Go on; why not?"

Aldous shook his head, and moved his body about, searching for words in frustration.

"We humans are slaves to our preconceptions. It's hard for us to learn, and almost impossible for us to unlearn. I don't know how well I've put that."

Gulliver stood frozen. At last, he said, "I'm going to have to study the human brain." He held up his hand, then, in a quick decision, pushed the button on his watch.

Urgent. Gulliver reporting:

Human brain is rigid in preconceptions. Very difficult to learn the new, almost impossible to unlearn. End.

Gulliver visibly relaxed.

Aldous exclaimed, exasperated, "You should land on the White House lawn. There's nothing I can tell you.'

Gulliver said grimly, "I'm certainly going to scan Clinton's mind, but back home there's an agreement on what I may find. You're the one man I need. I can't talk telepathically with anyone else."

Aldous said firmly, "I'm on holiday, and I want to get back to my canoe trip."

Gulliver said, with reproval, "You haven't listened. Eleven days have passed. You are expected in Pickle Creek, to hand in your ATV."

"Damn you! You've made me lose a much-needed holiday, with all its exercise!"

"You've never felt so well in your life. Your muscles are stronger, and. we've rejuvenated your cells. Brother, dear, what ingratitude."

Aldous took a deep breath, then gave a wry grin.

"Have you woken up Susan?"

"Not yet."

"So how will you explain your presence?'

"We'll take you back to your log cabin. I'll walk around Pickle Creek, and 'run into' the owner of your ATV. He'll think I'm you. When we get that cleared up, I'll hire a motorbike, and ride down to your cabin. Why? Because all these. years I've known I've had a brother. Your three brothers were born of your mother's second marriage in Canada. Your father was English, from Wiltshire. He had a secret love, in England, and I am the result. My mother told me I had a half-brother – that my father had married someone else, but I didn't have a clue as to finding my brother. Now in Pickle Creek, this Canadian tells me that my spitting image is in this log cabin close by, so off I go to investigate on a motorcycle. Susan will witness the incredible reunion."

"What post-hypnotic suggestion are you going to plant on Susan?"

"She'll wake up in her bunk in the cabin, remembering a marvellous two weeks canoeing up into Bluestone Lake and Bamoki Lake."

Aldous shook his head.

"When you turn up at the cabin, I'm not going to be able to act the part – that you're my long lost brother and I'm seeing you for the first time."

"I'll hypnotise you, brother dear, never fear, you're in the best of hands."

Aldous glared at him.

"What are your strongest emotions, back where you live?"

Gulliver said, "Love. Humour. We have a powerful sense of the incongruous, and love the incongruous in all its forms. But we feel love to each other."

"And sex?"

"We have two sexes, to reproduce. But we don't have sexual attraction, sexual pleasure, sexual passion. Very disappointing, old boy."

Aldous sat, deep in thought. Finally, he asked, "One last question. How the hell does that scooter disc of yours work?"

"Well," said Gulliver slowly, thinking, "Imagine a closed, circular pipe running around the inside circumference of the disc, against the outer edge, but inside the walls of course. Imagine molten metal alloy spinning around inside at high speed. That sets up all sorts useful fields, and does the job very well."

Aldous nodded sagely.

On the plane to Thunder Bay, and on the flight from Thunder Bay to Toronto, Susan could not stop – the marvel, the miracle of it. "Your half-brother, after all these years! In that tiny town!"

With resignation, he went to his flat in Carlton St. Gulliver might not be there. But as he drew near, he sensed him in the distance.

Gulliver opened the door for him, beaming.

"Brother Aldous," he smiled. "Home at last. Are you hungry?"

"Not at all," said Aldous tiredly.

"Let me help you with that stuff."

Half-an-hour later, when Aldous had unpacked, Gulliver said, with great charm, "I desperately need your help."

"Count on it," said Aldous automatically.

"I have seen from your memories that Susan has bikes. I'd like to take a spin around Missassauga and see upon what far shore I've fetched up. My knowledge is really beyond your earthern imagining –"

"*Earthly!*" sighed Aldous. "Earthly!"

"Your earthly imagining, but here I am in the curious position of ignorance. I want you to receive a large number of consultations, so I can listen in telepathically from the next room, and find out about you humans..."

"I don't have *that* many consultations –"

"I'll bring them into you, telepathically. I'll trawl for you, and you'll make a mint."

"All right," said Aldous, drumming his fingers. "Would you like to take a spin on the bikes?"

"Sure. We'll have to take a train. At first it runs underground –"

"Ah! The Underground. The Metro. All your machinery is educational."

* * *

They took the GO train, and got out at Dixie, then strolled towards Susan's.

"What a beautiful place," said Gulliver.

"Don't judge the planet by this," warned Aldous. "In summer, these are perhaps the most beautiful suburbs in the world. Down in Australia, you've got the garden suburbs of Melbourne, but they're all broken up by fences."

They went along a street with gardens and fences.

Aldous sent, "Don't judge it all by streets like this. Many streets are like parks, without any fences."

Aldous spoke out loud, "How long do you live?"

"We never die. We grow tens of thousands of bodies and store them. If there's an accident, we just 'walk into' a new body. When we get tired, we go back to the First Dimension."

"If the First Dimension is heaven, why leave it at all? What am I doing, here on earth?"

"Don't you ever go to the cinema? Don't you watch stories on television? Dramas, comedies? Don't you read novels? To come into this Universe is a sort of game. It's to go to the cinema. The other dimensions don't have hard surfaces, lumps – here you've got rocks, planets, stars, galaxies – streets, houses. You come here to enjoy yourself."

"Not on this planet, you don't."

Gulliver stopped dead, and stared at him intently.

"Why not?"

"People inflict atrocious suffering on each other. Circumstances beat you down. That's why I do my Readings for people. To help them see the future, and reduce their suffering."

"If you can't see the future, how do you do *anything*?"

"By trial and error. The greatest philosopher of this century, Karl Popper, reminded us that we must never forget our limitations. That everything we do is by trial and error. We look at the past, and try and guess the future from it."

"Please," said Gulliver. He pressed his watch, and transmitted:

Urgent. Gulliver reporting:

Human activities governed by trial and error. Cannot see the future. Judge the past to guess at the future. End.

Aldous nodded his approval. "That's us in a nutshell," he said morosely. "Can't you use another word than that silly 'Urgent'?"

"'Urgent' is just my translation for a signal that my message has priority for the Supreme Committees and the Grand Council. They'll be shaking their heads over this. Your human dilemma boils down to your not being able to see the future. I have seen that you have fathered thirty-two psychic children. That's nothing! Couldn't you father tens of thousands?"

"Impossible. I'd need total cooperation."

"How many psychics are there?"

"Hundreds of thousands. But most have a feeble gift. True, powerful psychics – I dunno, say, a couple of hundred."

"Couldn't they donate sperm, and each use their gifts to tell a hundred thousand women when to fertilize? You could change the genetic constitution of the race in a few generations."

"God, the rest of the men would slaughter us! There's what's known as your Selfish Gene, remember? In our animal kingdom, I must admit, the males try to make their genes prevail over those of other males. A pride of lions will have lion cubs, and they lose their male. The new male will kill all the cubs, and sire its own. Elephant herds, as with so many animals, allow only females, and they raise the offspring. Males can join them only to copulate, and then they're kicked out."

Gulliver had stopped, staring at him.

"So that's why there're all these wars we see on Television?"

"We humans are above that!"

"Please, just a minute."

He pressed his watch, and sent:

Urgent. Gulliver reporting:

Humans behave like animals and are governed by the Selfish Gene. Mates try to slaughter mates. One reason for the unending wars. End.

Aldous took a few hesitant steps, and Gulliver followed him. Aldous said, "It's more complicated than that. Animals have a Territorial Instinct – well, carnivores, monkeys and birds. We're descended from monkeys. Carnivores go around peeing on trees to mark the land that belongs to them. A lot of wars are fought just for territory, because I read somewhere that part of our brain is animal."

Gulliver drew a sharp breath. "Indeed! We must go to London, so that I can get into the British Library there, or whatever it is. The British Museum Library?"

"You'll not get in. You need recommendations, I don't know what else!"

Gulliver grinned wickedly. "I'll hypnotise the minds of the men guarding the gates. No problem, I assure you. I'm going to have to read all about the human brain."

Aldous said, "In Kosovo, part of the problem were some rich mineral deposits. But the real reason was the Serbian territorial instinct. That's just my private opinion. When Bangladesh wanted free of Pakistan, there were one million deaths. Bangladesh is about the poorest country in the world, but Pakistan still wanted to keep it. Land! Land! Land! There were photos of Pakistani soldiers bayoneting civilians, with crowds standing round. The photos were atrocious – the agony on the faces of the victims on the ground. All those civilians wanted was an independent Bangladesh. The soldiers doing the bayoneting had to have animal minds. A rational man cannot bayonet another man."

Gulliver stopped again, and took a deep breath. "I must impose again on your patience, Aldous."

He pressed his watch, and said:

Urgent. Gulliver sending:

Humans have animal territorial instinct and will kill millions in wars for territory. End.

"Succinct," said Aldous. "Succinct. I suppose I could qualify that. In the past, in agricultural societies, land meant crops and food. In the American Civil War, and the wars since then, conquest could mean gaining industry, coal and iron mines – you know what I mean?"

"I take your point all too well," said Gulliver grimly.

* * *

Susan greeted Gulliver excitedly, and said, "Of course you can take the bikes."

Scanning her, Aldous realised that, with feminine perversity, she felt Gulliver was an underdog, and the fault was of Aldous' father, and of Aldous himself."

Gulliver read her like an open book. He said, "Could we practise in your back garden? There were no bikes for me when I was a boy..."

Susan exploded, "Of course you can! Aldous will teach you," and she gave Aldous a hard look.

"A pleasure," said Aldous darkly, while Gulliver gave her a trusting smile of one who has found a mother surrogate.

For fifteen minutes, Aldous had to run around in circles, while Gulliver followed, seated on the bike, one hand on Aldous' shoulder. Gulliver sent, "While I was popping in and out of this Dimension, I should have learnt. I don't know how to apologise."

Aldous panted, "Then don't try."

* * *

Out on the street, they pedalled for some minutes and picked up Bloor St. They got off that, because of cars, and took Ivernia Rd to Flagship Drive, then down Rymal Road to a Lane which put them on Dundas St. They left that on Tedlo St. for Orwell St, and rode into Cawthra Rd., which they followed to Atwater Ave. By back streets, they reached Elizabeth St, which put them onto Lakeshore Rd to cross the Credit River.

Street after street would often stretch before them half a kilometre –

each street a park of intense green. On either side, grass verges lined the roadway, verges planted with trees, with a concrete pavement behind. And beyond the pavement lay the gardens, but without fences, so that the gardens ran on as a park. Each garden had ten or twenty tall trees, all different. One house stood close, half seen among the trees; the next was so far back they caught a fleeting glimpse only. The streets were a riot of green.

They came up against river and creek beds, and detoured onto streets that crossed them, riding into Oakville and Milton.

Gulliver was whooping and laughing.

"Look at this," he cried. "I can't believe it. It's fantastic. Look at those people walking along! If they knew someone was riding past them on a bike, who had come from thirty light years away. And if they could just see me now back in Xhemptuw! If they could just!"

They saw two people approaching.

"Just imagine they knew I was Zuxkirw!"

"No problem," said Aldous, pedalling hard to keep up. "Their preconceptions would protect them."

Gulliver sent, "I hope you haven't exaggerated this of the preconceptions!"

Aldous was too short of breath to speak. Instead, he sent, "Do you want an example? In the Second World War, the Germans had to depend on their submarines to bring down Great Britain – to starve it out, on the high seas... okay, the British discover radar in the meter bands, and begin zeroing in on the U-boats. The U-boats install apparatus which register the British radar beams, and dive when they realise they've been 'seen'. Next thing, no more radar beams. British planes spring upon surfaced U-boats and sink them, drowning their crews like rats. British warships close on surfaced U-boats, which dive too late, and are sunk by depth-charge. Scores and scores of U-boats sunk, Germany's losing the war and supplies pour into Britain. The British have an unknown weapon! At the beginning of 1942, German captain Meckel insists the British have radar in the centimetre band, but German scientists say that's impossible, They had tried that a couple of years before and got a weak, confused signal. Right through 1942 and 1943, sinkings of U-boats accelerate and Meckel says, 'let's build just one receptor for the centimetre band and try it out at sea!' Permission refused, because radar in the centimetre band is impossible. In January, 1944, a British bomber crashes in Rotterdam. With agonising care and trouble, the Germans rebuilt its radar set – and, lo and behold! the bomber's radar set is working on the 10-centimetre band! By that time, losing the war at sea, Germany had lost the war, because now it had two fronts – an intact Britain, and Russia."

Gulliver slowed down, and said, "I don't believe you." By this time, they had gone up Wesley Ave and Kane Rd to Indian Rd.

"If you don't like the evidence, then go back to your planet."

50

"No conscious, intelligent mind behaves like that. Not in our quadrant of the galaxy, not in any quadrant."

"Just as you heard it."

"Then the human mind has suffered grave evolutionary impairment, it's defective, it's flawed."

"I reckon that about describes us."

They rode on to South Sheridan way, to get across Queen Elizabeth Way. They finally picked up the 5th Line West, and then explored Blue Beech Crescent and Buttonhush Crescent. They made their way to Windjammer Rd., and explored the Crescents around King Masting Park.

"Mind you," ventured Aldous, "The most important activity of human beings is to seek status. It's in their minds all day long."

Gulliver sent, "All this around here is so beautiful. One house Tudor, the next mock Spanish, the next ante-Bellum Virginian, the next Tyrolean, the next Gothic... does this represent status?"

"You bet it does! But status can come with money, power, academic or artistic distinctions – with bluff. The way you dress. In Britain, you get it cheap with your accent. Those without status depend on love – you're loved despite being a nobody, just being a housewife."

"So that's the niche for love in human dealings," sighed Gulliver.

"When a man is sexually attracted to a desirable woman, he tells he 'loves' her. Men tell women they 'love' them, all the time, because that's what women most want to hear. Women interpret that to mean that a man will separate himself from his resources and give them to *her*."

Gulliver stopped and got off his hike. He pressed his watch, and transmitted:

Urgent. Gulliver reporting:

Humans obsessed every hour with their status. Depends on money, power, distinction. Love is negotiable. End.

"How does that watch work?"

"There's a small robot hovering about three hundred feet above our heads. It not only transmits hut also protects me. If a car were about to hit me, it would vaporise the car. Very useful. Really, everyone should have one."

He walked heavily along the street, and said, "I'm worried and upset. I must get to that famous Library in London." He stopped in front of a house, and said, "What's that number for?"

"We send messages written on paper. If you put the country, the city, the street, and then the number of the house, it gets delivered by hand."

"Cumbersome."

"Now we have a worldwide electronic net, and we send messages that way too. Or we send electronic signals which we convert back to sound, so you can hear someone talking on the other side of the world."

Gulliver gave a heavy sigh. "Just a moment." He pressed his watch.

Urgent. Gulliver reporting:

Humans have worldwide electronic net. Transmits visuals or voice. End.

He said, "Well, let's head hack."

Aldous said, "I'm getting hungry. Let's go."

Riding along at the speed Gulliver kept up, Aldous, to save his breath, sent, "People go into politics and become leaders because that's the highest status. Some leaders somehow get control of a country's mind, and people follow them like slaves. Hitler did it in Germany. In this collective frenzy, people go to war, as they did in the Second World War, and 50,000,000 people end up dead."

Gulliver put on his brakes, and got off his bike. He pressed his watch, and said:

Urgent. Gulliver reporting:

Some leaders exploit an incomprehensible factor in human brain to make them slaves to his will, and then up to 50,000,000 get killed. Will study human brain in depth. It is an evolutionary failure and abnormal. End.

Gulliver said apologetically, "I do hope you don't think I'm being rude. No aspersions on *your* brain, my dear brother. Thankfully, you seem different to the others."

"I've never killed anyone," mused Aldous, as they mounted their hikes. "But I will say this – basically, every man wants to kill all other men, given half a chance. Thank God, the chances are few and far between, here in the West."

"Oh, dear," said Gulliver, getting off his bike again, and propping it up. "I'll accept that statement of yours, because the evidence is overwhelming. Remember, we have been getting forty years of your television programs and documentaries, which, truth be told, we found utterly

incomprehensible, all the violence."
He pressed his watch.

Urgent. Gulliver reporting:
All human males basically want to kill all other males.

Back home in his flat in Carlton St, Aldous gave the second bedroom to Gulliver.

Next morning, the first visitor arrived, and as always, Aldous used the living-room.

The man had a thin, drawn face, and wore an old suit, with a shirt and tie. He sat uneasily in the chair, gnawed his lip, and said, "I'm forty-one and an accountant. I feel my life is empty, pointless."

He didn't look Aldous in the face, and entwined his fingers.

"I'd like to do something else, but I have no idea. I need my income from the job I have... well, you know –"

Aldous said, "You have a son and daughter at University, and your wife doesn't work."

After a long pause, Aldous said, "This is not the sort of Reading I do."

The man gave him a depressed look, and Aldous said, "Let me sit and think."

They sat, the minutes passing, Aldous perfectly still, and man fidgeting.

"Well," said Aldous. "I do see something. You can look for another job, as accountant, for half a day. You begin finding private clients – small firms to do accountancy for. Then, you go back to school and do carpentry. I see two years training. By then, you will have private clients, giving you two-thirds of your present income. You go back to school to study joinery and furniture-making. I see two more years of that, and you are accepted by a master furniture maker called Larry, who will be 63 years old. He will teach you. He is a master. I see furniture of Louis XIV, Louis XV, Louis XVI, Chippendale, Adam... I don't know furniture, hut I see these names confusedly. Larry will retire. You can buy out his Goodwill, but you will do better paying him a monthly pension. It will be a very good market..."

A patch of perspiration had formed on Aldous' shirt front, and drops of perspiration showed on his face.

He said, "That is all."

The man looked at him lugubriously, then said, "You may be right."

For the first time, he smiled, and took out his wallet and paid Aldous.

After the man left, Gulliver came in from next door and sat down heavily. "I'm amazed," he said. "How can anyone live without knowing what

54

the future offers? Where would that chap be without you? I admit I'm confused, nonplussed, horrified. All of this is so new −"

Aldous said, "I wasn't sure I could handle it. How does this gift work?"

"You tap into the First Dimension. You have neurons of a certain composition that can catch the energy wavelengths. Go and change your shirt. Someone else's coming."

* * *

The next visitor was a lady, comfortably dressed, with an inexpensive handbag. She had been to the hairdressers, had sensible shoes, and wore glasses.

She sat down matter-of-factly and said, straightforward, "I am forty-one and I'm pregnant. We have one son of 18 and another of ten. Could I ask you some questions?"

Aldous smiled. "You are here to ask questions."

"If the baby is born, will it be all right, despite my age?"

Aldous nodded.

"By the time the baby is twenty, I'll be sixty-one. Will I be able to cope?"

Aldous shook his head. "No," he said. "You will have trouble with your spinal disks. You husband will be made redundant. You will suffer income loss, but your eldest son will help, till you collect your pensions. You will not be able to finance a third child."

The lady sagged, and lost her self-assurance.

"What can I do about the back problem?"

Aldous sat in silence, unable to answer.

He heard Gulliver in his mind. 'Tell her to go to a gym and do exercises for her back, every day of her life.'

Aldous repeated the words.

The woman looked at him wordlessly, smiled uncertainly, and paid him.

* * *

Gulliver came out after she had left and said, "I'm at a total loss. No one can be expected to live like this. These are the lucky ones, but what about the rest?"

Aldous went to the bathroom, and splashed his face. He was worried about Claude.

What could he tell Claude about Gulliver? He agonised over it.

That Aldous' father had married and divorced before marrying Beatrice, his own mother and mother of Claude? When Aldous' father died, Beatrice had remarried in Canada and had three more sons – Claude, George and Phil. Claude had a sober, staid streak. To hear that his mother had married some divorced man hack in England would fluster... then mortify him. He would control his anger against Aldous, but would see ignominy everywhere.

* * *

He was solidly-built, about twenty-seven, with a bony face and big hands.

"I'm a handyman," he said. "Plumbing, electricity, you know. Years ago I had a baby with my girlfriend, Janet, but then she fell in love with someone else, and got me to sign away my rights. So, she gets married, see, but now – she's divorced, and she's coming back at me for maintenance of the boy.

"But, meanwhile, I got married, and have two children. If I pay maintenance, that's going to affect our standard of living, and my wife's round the bend over it. We've got a mortgage, and other payments on top of that. My wife may have to go to work – go to work to pay the money to another woman! My wife and I aren't going to last long on that basis!"

He stopped expectantly, hitting the flat of one hand against the fist of the other.

Aldous held up his hand, while he thought and searched.

"The mother of your first child is seeking revenge – is seeking to destroy you and your wife. So long as you pay her, she will never remarry, and your first son will be without a father, without any stepfather. Your boy will grow up to be moody, but with a stepfather he'll study and get an education. If you make the payments, you and your wife will break up, and your children by this marriage will have a bad upbringing, without their father. Your first son eventually – well, he'll marry an understanding wife. But the other two children won't do so well. I see the problem solving itself if you sell up your house, and move down to, say, Florida. Work at your job, but don't put in for Social Security so you can't be traced. Put everything in your wife's name, so no claim can be made against your goods. No credit cards or vehicles in your name. I see the mother of your first son making a search for you, which will be unsuccessful at first. Then she will remarry, and the search will cease. After four years, you can go back into Social Security..."

The man nodded.

"That's pretty clear. Thanks."

He paid Aldous.

* * *

After he left, Gulliver came out, and said, "These people try to handle the past, the present and future at the same time. But if you're not here to tell them about the future, it's all ifs and buts and no certain answers. And everyone is mired in these desperate ambiguities, these hopeless quests. It looks to me as though most people just have to sit there and take what is dished out. We're dealing with consciousness! the light of all existence, and it's muddied and blinded and tormented on this planet beyond all recognition."

* * *

She was about twenty-four, an angular woman, smartly dressed, and moved with quick energy. She sat down decidedly, smiled at him brightly, and said, "My mother's driving me nuts. She keeps on and on at me. Mind you, she's got a neurotic problem, but when she interferes in my marriage, I find that pretty serious. The problem is, my husband and I like to have things *out*! We don't bottle things up – when we don't agree, we argue; when one of us is worried, that one argues; when we don't like something that's been done – or is going to be done – we argue. I feel we've got a healthy, *vigorous* relationship, where nobody crawls away and hides things. But my mother! When I was seven, she got divorced. Apparently, she and my father never raised their voices – it was all sweetie-pie, till my father walked out, and I've never seen him to this day. Look where it got my mother – bottling it all up!

"But my mother never leaves me in peace. All my arguments with my husband – we're a marriage on the rocks, we're going to bust up! My marriage won't last!

"I want you to tell me what's going to happen, and then if I can persuade my mother to ring you, I wonder whether you could repeat to her whatever you tell me."

She stared at him intently.

"Because my marriage is going to be okay, isn't it? It's going to last, isn't it?"

Aldous smiled and nodded.

"You'll have three children. You'll celebrate your Silver and Golden

57

Anniversaries. You'll have five grandchildren, and I don't know how many great-grandchildren."

"You wonderful man!" she shrieked. She jumped up, leant over and kissed Aldous on the cheek.

"This is my card, and I've written my mother's name on the top. I don't want to have to break with my mother, but if she won't ring you, or won't believe you, then I'll have done everything that it's in my power to do."

Aldous smiled again.

"Your mother will ring me. She won't be entirely convinced, but she will be sufficiently satisfied to stop making so many remarks. I can tell you she will find the news —" he laughed — "intimidating enough to make her measure her words."

She paid him, squeezed his hand, and left.

* * *

Gulliver came out, bemused.

*

"Well, at last, someone's happy. I'd given up on all of you. Can you tell me why she's happy? Because she's right and her mother's wrong? Or because her marriage will work when her mother's didn't? Or because she'll be able to argue for fifty years? With her husband, I take it? Or because she thinks she'll win all the arguments with him? Or because she thinks being married for fifty years is the best thing that can happen?"

"Not the slightest idea."

"What do you think makes people happy, Aldous?"

"There's no answer to that. For some people, it's sacrificing themselves. For others, it's grabbing what you can get. For some it's pleasure, for others, pain. For others, it a forcing themselves to their very limits. It's all those things, and about half a million more."

"Chaos confounded," grumbled Gulliver, and shook his head.

* * *

After lunch, the bell rang. He was young, thin, wiry, in shorts and a T-shirt, and he said, "I'm twenty-two and a student and I could be a bit out of my depth."

He looked at Aldous, ingenuously, and Aldous instantly distrusted the expression. "My parents have sent me here, and are paying for the Reading."

58

Aldous nodded.

"I keep getting into – well, serious, lengthy, meaningful love affairs. I take them pretty seriously, and I feel that my feelings have been powerfully reciprocated."

Aldous stared.

"Two of them," Aldous supplied.

The student looked at him in surprise.

"Well, I thought they were permanent, because one lasted eighteen months and the other for two years. That's an awful long time if you're living at my phase in your life."

Aldous looked solemn.

"I mention all of this so you understand I get *involved* – I don't just bang and scram."

"Yes," said Aldous, putting approval into his voice.

"Now, we had this back-packing trip up beyond Thunder Bay –"

Aldous blinked.

"– and in the woods we ran into this group, and I got talking to this – well, woman, very sexy, older than me – well, I sorta got her phone number here in Toronto – and – er, we've been seeing each other... well, we're lovers, and she's asked me to move in with her."

"And she's thirty—three," supplied. Aldous.

The boy's jaw dropped.

Aldous said, "So you're asking what a going to happen?"

The boy nodded.

"You're going to have a terrific sexual relationship. She's more mature, you're still young. Five times a night. She's working, and she'll help you finish your University. You'll get a job. When you turn thirty, she'll be forty-two, and you'll become acutely aware of her age. You'll meet this girl of nineteen..."

Aldous let his voice trail away.

Finally, the boy said, "I move in with this new girl?"

"That's it."

"What happens to my lover?"

"An emotional tailspin. Drinks too much, but she doesn't lose her job. Four years later, she meets a guy of fifty. He can't satisfy her. She picks up with a married man of thirty-two on the side, just for sex, and she marries the man of fifty."

"Gee, well that sounds all right," the student said finally. "I mean it ends without a... whimper." His voice trailed off.

Aldous looked at him steadily.

"You'll be all right, anyway."

Avoiding his eyes, the thin twenty-two year-old got up and paid him.

* * *

Gulliver came out, and offered hopefully, "I can vaporize his balls, quite painlessly.

"And I'll be the first one that they investigate," said Aldous balefully, and stared at Gulliver in alarm.

* * *

The woman was about fifty, conservatively dressed, a lined face. She walked slowly, and. sat down in the chair, giving Aldous a steady look, sizing him up. She favoured grey and pink-grey in her dress.

"I've come about my husband," she said.

Aldous said, "I know. He's fifty-eight, and he's ill."

"Well," said the lady. "Exactly."

Then she said, "Can you tell me what's going to happen? How much time have we left together?"

"Two years and two months."

"Will he suffer?"

"Not with the painkillers. In the hospital, keep after the nurses on the painkillers. He says he hurts, you go straight out looking for the nurses. You'll have three weeks in that hospital. He'll he conscious to the end, but it'll be easy for him because you'll be there, and he loves you. That will change everything."

She blinked several times, her hands in her lap.

"Thank you," she said, standing up, opening her purse and paying him. "I really need to know how much time we have left. I was afraid it might be only months. Knowing it will he longer means a lot to me."

After she left, Gulliver came in, and Aldous said, "Can you cure him?"

Gulliver said, "Easily, but I need permission." He pressed his watch.

Urgent. Gulliver reporting:
Request permission to cure dying man. End.

The reply came back a couple of hours later.

Supreme Committee to Gulliver:

60

No. End.

At their evening meal, Aldous asked Gulliver, "How come you got our electronic fingerprint, but we didn't get yours?"

"We don't use electronics. Maybe we did five hundred thousand years ago. Well, originally, as each of the nine planets got discovered it would be because of their electronic signals. But as each planet came into the Confederation, its science and technology was brought up to level."

"And only nine?"

"The Earth will make ten – although I'm beginning to wonder whether Earth will be admitted. Everything here is disquieting. Evolution seems to have gone haywire. Of course, we're just one quadrant of the galaxy, and tiny."

"And what about the UFOs?"

"We saw all about UFOs on your TV. Hysterical imagination."

Aldous shook his head.

"I was driving in the north of England, near the foothills of the Pennines. I saw this disc – about four o'clock in the afternoon, so I stopped the car and sent out a probe. What I got was a mind so *alien*, so utterly cold, foreign, grotesque – it threw up a block, and suddenly he hit me with a... a... savage probe. I blocked him, and tried for another crew member, and again I got this unearthly mind – nothing I could comprehend. He threw up a block, and the disc veered sharply, moved at an incredible speed and stopped above me, at about five hundred feet height. My car engine was idling, and it stopped. They bombarded my mind, but I blocked them easily. I found a way through one of their blocks, and again got this incomprehensible consciousness. Some seconds after I did that, the disc vanished."

"WHAT!" cried Gulliver, getting to his feet.

He paced up and down the room, agitated, his hands shaking and his lips trembling. Then he took control of himself, breathed deeply several times, and forced himself to sit down.

"Aldous, tomorrow you've got that haunted house, right? I can't come with you. I've got to go to the Toronto Public Library. Can you draw me a sketch, how to get there?"

"My dear brother, need you ask? Tell me, how did the disc vanish like that?"

"Whipped back into the Fourth," said Gulliver absently. "You know, back into the Fourth Dimension. That's why no one here takes them seriously – suddenly appearing, suddenly vanishing. They're popping in and popping out from the Fourth."

Next morning, Aldous took the SL and H train to Meadowvale Station, and walked along Acquitaine Ave, then turned off and looked for the address he had written down. He found himself among Crescents, then saw the house, went in, and rang the bell.

A woman of about twenty-eight opened it. Her hair was in a pony-tail, blonde. She looked at him with blue eyes, from a creamy-skinned, unlined face. Her clothes were casual and expensively cut. Aldous supposed most wives around there would be working, but this one was lucky.

"Mr. Windsor."

"Thank God you've come! I'm Mrs. Shields. Come in."

The wide, cream hall impressed Aldous. Inside, two Ionic columns flanked the front door. On each side of the circular room was set an alcove, with two more columns. She led him through a door into a long living-room, done in mahogany panelling and dark leather, with bookcases. Surpassing interior decoration. Aldous pursed his lips in admiration.

She sat him in a deep, padded, leather armchair. "Doesn't look like a haunted house," he smiled.

She said, "I'm taking it as understood that I can rely on your discretion and silence. If any of the neighbours knew about this – my God! I can imagine what they'd think of me."

"I can give you an absolute and total guarantee on that. If that weren't the case, nobody could talk to me. You can't begin to imagine the secrets I hear."

"Yes, it's obvious when you think about it."

She studied him, and took a deep breath.

"In this house, there's my husband and two daughters, the eldest eight, the other seven. All of us have heard and seen what's happening. Normally, you couldn't hope to make two small girls keep a secret, but they're so frightened..."

Aldous jumped to his feet. A woman stepped through the wall at the back of the room and stood looking at him. She was young, beautiful, with a certain family likeness to Mrs. Shields. Aldous guessed she was dressed in the fashion of the nineteen-thirties.

Aldous said, "Your ghost has just entered the room. She's wearing a long, tube-like dress, that looks like a way of dressing in the nineteen-thirties."

Mrs. Shields swung around to look, giving a strangled cry.

She gasped, "I can't see anything."

"Do you have photos of your grandparents?"

"Yes, I do. They're dead."

The woman who had come through the wall stood looking at him, and then walked across the room and stood in front of him.

Aldous sent, "Who are you?"

No reply.

He probed and found emptiness, silence.

Aldous said, "She's crossed the room and now she's standing right in front of me. She won't speak to me."

The woman walked to a door, stood there, and looked over her shoulder at Aldous. Aldous went over to her, then opened the door. She led him down a passage to the kitchen, which had the door open.

Mrs. Shields, very frightened, followed at a distance.

Aldous stood in the centre of the kitchen, while the woman stood beside the outer door. Mrs. Shields stood in the doorway Aldous had just crossed.

Annoyed, Aldous suddenly exclaimed, "What is it you want?"

The woman stood there.

Suddenly Aldous saw an explosion envelop the room, followed by a sea of flames. He saw the walls and ceiling collapse, engulfed by flames.

Slowly, the flames died away and he saw the kitchen again. The woman stood looking at him, then vanished.

Aldous swung around and looked at Mrs. Shields. "She's gone. She came to give you a message. There will be a big explosion in this kitchen and the whole house will burn."

She turned white and leaned against the door frame, then recovered and led him back to the sitting-room.

"May I see those photos?"

She opened a dark-panelled door, and took out several albums, chose one, and handed it to him.

He saw fading black-and-white snaps from the thirties. Then he saw a

63

photo – it was the woman who had appeared to him.

He showed it to Mrs. Shields.

She said, "That's my maternal grandmother."

Then she asked him, "How will the explosion happen?"

They went back to the kitchen, and he probed. After four minutes, he turned to a door and opened it. It held the tall heating apparatus, which took up almost all the cupboard.

"Your fuel tank is under the house, is it?"

She nodded.

"Something is wrong with a pipe leading up from the tank, and something else is wrong too. Get men in to check it. If they don't find two serious faults, throw it out and install a completely new heater with new piping. Or call in a second firm to check it. You have to find two serious faults, and if not, get rid of it."

He had been sweating, and his shirt stuck to him. She paid him, and he left.

* * *

Gulliver came in flustered, twitching his fingers.

"Gulliver, that ghost was a grandmother from the nineteen-thirties, who came to warn them that the house would blow up. How could she get out of the First Dimension?"

Gulliver said, "If she's a High Spirit, she can cross over. We all can on my planet – well, all of us on the nine planets. If she is a Higher Spirit, she can cross over and make herself seen to ordinary people."

He sat down, drumming his fingers.

"Before we have lunch, I have to send a very long message."

"What I'm damned if I understand is why you send them in English."

"Because I've got a human voice box, and English is the language programmed into my brain. The robot transmits it to the yacht, and the yacht transcribes it. No problem".

"Do you want me to bring you coffee, so your voice box doesn't go dry?"

Gulliver smiled, and said, "Let's make coffee and then I'll begin."

Urgent. Gulliver reporting:

Message of utmost magnitude. UFO sightings are not human imaginings.

Human with psychic capacity probed a disc and found utterly alien minds. Disc approached a high speed, hovered over him at 500 feet. Occupants sent a 'savage' probe which he countered. He probed them, and they countered. He overcame their block, and disc vanished.

Obviously, discs enter and leave the Fourth Dimension. The sudden appearances and disappearances explain humans discounting and even ridiculing the sightings.

THESE ALIENS HAVE NOT CONTACTED THE HUMANS. THEY HAVE NOT OFFERED TO RAISE THE SCIENTIFIC AND TECHNOLOGICAL LEVEL HERE. SUSPECT QUARANTINE.

Have discovered recent sightings not reported on the popular TV:

a)   Positive identification. Medium yacht, a disc shape, one kilometre diameter, emerged from the Fourth and was spotted by aircrew flying at 11,700 metres. Also caught on ground radar for 50 seconds. Without observed visual movement, it disappeared before the eyes of aircrew and vanished from radar screen at same moment i.e. went back into the Fourth Dimension.

b)　　　March 8, 1995, a military radar screen near Lucern in Switzerland picked up the track of an UFO, as it emerged suddenly from the Fourth. Followed a straight line in descent from 21.7 km to some 6.2 km, as seen on the military screen, and on other screens for covering civilian air traffic, over some 240 km. Speed almost Mach 3, when Mach 2 is the legal top speed for high-performance planes over Europe.

First spotted when the disc was about 430 km from the radar screen, the radar station standing at 2.1 km altitude above sea level. The radar apparatus got four 'hits' at ten second pauses (beam rotated at 6 revolutions per minute), and that gives us segment number one. Then the radar stopped tracking it. But during these 30 seconds, the object descended from 21.7 km to 19.8 km altitude, and covered about 28 km distance, putting it at 402 km from the station.

The radar measured speeds of 3,348, 3,358, 3,356 and 3,368 km an hour in four different 'takes'.

These earthly radar installations work by rules which decide what's to be tracked and what isn't. After a few registrations, the system automatically stops 'seeing' objects above a certain height, or that go faster than a certain speed, or that zigzag too much, and so on. Basically, they are looking for normal aircraft and blocking out everything else. So, after the first four markings, the system phased out this object, probably because of extraordinary speed.

So, for 70 seconds it flew on, undetected. Then the Lucern radar and a second, military radar reinterpreted it as being a 'new' object, at some 335 km from Lucern. So, it was tracked again for six rotations. Two tracks of some kilometres apart were registered, although it was really only one object. This time, the radars took six 'hits', each radar measuring it at about 3,360 km an hour. The object went on losing height, from about 15.7 km to 13.1 km as it travelled some 47 km in a straight line.

However, this second sighting lines up perfectly with the earlier, first sighting. It travelled in a straight line from one set of 'hits' to the next.

So, for a second time, the system rejected the object, and stopped tracking it.

A minute later, Lucern radar 'saw' another 'new' object, now at 228 km from the radar screen. Then, over 140 seconds, the object was picked up, lost and then picked up three more times, before the radar dumped it for a third and final time at 190 km from the radar screen. It had lost altitude, descending from 7.7km height to 6.2 km, while the object covered another 38 km distance. Average speed was about 3,400 km an hour. Doppler velocities from the radar itself gave 3,392 km to 3,326 km an hour.

Your Excellencies, an object was detected which covered some 240 km in some 250 seconds, which gives us a speed of some 3,456 km an hour.

Between the first two segments which it registered, it did about 3,446 km an hour, and between the second and third stretches, it ran at about 3,600 km an hour, these speeds being higher than the speeds given by the radars. It was levelling out after a fast descent, and finally was doing Mach 2.75 at only 6.2 km height – totally illegal in European airspace.

I am ruling out atmospheric refraction giving false radar returns. Refraction bends down some radar beams so they reflect objects on the ground at fixed points. That means we must rule out buildings, moving road traffic and. mountain tops. Also, we have to rule out detection of a high-speed aircraft flying close to the ground. The cross-section of a high-speed jet flying straight at the radar station is about two square meters – or less! – and at 430 km, the radar needs a cross-section of six square meters. At 500 km, radar needs ten square meters. So, the radar could not have picked a jet that far away – not at the distance it did pick up this UFO.

The track ended suddenly, as the object drove back into the Fourth Dimension. Ordinary aircraft would have landed at Geneva, or if he had continued across Switzerland, the radars would have followed him – meaning the alien.

The trick of darting in and out of the Fourth is a total success. Almost all players in military and government disbelieve the reports. For the puny human brain, something cannot just vanish.

Why should they make this flight? To test earthly radar? An advanced civilisation does not fly over an Indian village deep in the Amazon jungle to find out how many bows and arrows they have.

What is clear is that they have not reached the technical level OF ENTERING THE THIRD DIMENSION. THEY CANNOT CLONE HUMAN BEINGS AND TAKE THE EMBRYO BACK 20 OR 30 YEARS IN THE THIRD FOR QUICK GROWTH AS I HAVE DONE. There are many reports of abduction and trying cross-fertilisation between humans and aliens, apparently without success.

This is an advanced planet or advanced Confederation in another quadrant.

Have they set up a robotised quarantine shield beyond the Oort Cloud?

c)   Another definite sighting:

On December 31, 1978, at ten minutes after midnight a UFO apparently jumped out of the Fourth over the coast of New Zealand.

A freighter plane, a 4-engine Argosy, flew from Wellington to Christchurch and made the sightings.

The first witness was the captain of the plane, with 23 years of experience. He had logged 14,000 hours of flying time. The second witness was the co-pilot, with 7,000 hours experience. The next witnesses were a TV reporter, a TV cameraman, and a sound recorder.

Your Excellencies on the Grand Council, and on the planetary Supreme Committees, could not be better served.

In fact, the TV crew was on board *because* of UFO sightings on previous days – visual and radar sightings – by air crews and radar operators.

Two months before, in October, a young pilot, Federick Valentich, was flying over Bass Strait and reported a bright object hovering over his plane. He vanished, and this caused a worldwide sensation.

I must suggest, with great foreboding, that he was kidnapped. These aliens have the technology to keep him alive, but for what reason? Or they caused the electrical system of his plane to fail, which indicates ineptitude and a threatening attitude incompatible with their technical level.

The New Zealand radars monitor traffic over 100 miles, and use vertical beams with 51 cm wavelength. The radar can be bent down to 'see' the coast.

The plane flew over Wellington at midnight, and ten minutes later turned left. The plane flew through a CAVU sky – that is, 'clear and visibility unlimited'. This means that a bright light could be spotted more than a hundred miles away. Aircrew saw the lights reaching down to Christchurch about 150 miles away.

Five minutes after midnight, the captain and co-pilot noticed erratic lights ahead of them. As they knew the coastal lights by heart, these lights were something else. The lights leapt out of the Fourth, projected a light downwards on the sea, and leapt back again. Or the lights were switched on and off. Sometimes one light, sometimes several. The captain and co-pilot wondered whether a search was under way.

Twelve minutes past midnight, they called WATCC radar, where there was a controller and mechanic on duty. At that moment, the plane was cruising at 215 nautical miles an hour at its proper altitude of 14,000 feet. The co-pilot had the controls, so the captain asked the radar about other planes in the air ahead of them.

The controller was tied up landing a plane, but for half an hour he had been noticing targets appearing and disappearing from his screen.

So, I believe they were jumping in and out of the Fourth, not simply switching lights on and off.

The controller told the captain, "There are targets in your one o'clock position at, uh, 13 miles, appearing and disappearing..."

Your Excellencies, the other plane landed, so that then the Argosy was alone in the sky.

Fifteen minutes past midnight, the radar station reported a target at about 3.00 on the coastline. The TV crew had been down in the cargo hold filming a discussion of the sightings, and came up to the flight deck where the aircrew pointed out to them the unusual lights through the windscreen. No one could see the target at three o' clock.

The TV crew had a battle on the flight deck – it was crowded and rowdy, and the cameraman was doing a balancing act with his heavy Bolex 16 mm electric camera with a 100 mm zoom and big film magazine on his shoulder while he squatted in a small chair between the captain on his left side and the co-pilot. So, he could film straight ahead through the windscreen, and not very well to the side. They gave him earphones. Sometimes, he would yell over all the noise to the reporter, on foot behind the co-pilot, to tell him what the WATCC was saying. The sound recordist crouched behind the cameraman with her tape recorder on the deck. They couldn't see anything, as she recorded the reporter while he described what he was seeing through the right window and through the front window, and she began to get scared at what he was saying.

One minute later they got their first sighting that was a definite. Radar transmitted, "Target briefly appeared at your twelve o'clock at 10 miles." The captain said, "Thank you," looked ahead, and saw a light in the middle of nowhere, The captain described the light as, "...white and not very brilliant and it did not change colour or flicker. To me, it looked like the taillight of an aircraft. I'm not sure how long we saw this for. Probably not very long."

The target was not seen on the next radar sweep, 12 seconds later.

The UFO whipped in and out of the Fourth and WATCC radar broadcast 20 seconds later, "...strong target showing at 11.00 at 3 miles."

Four radar rotations later i.e. 48 seconds later, WATCC told the plane, "just left of you at 9.00 at 2 miles." The captain stared out of his left window at nine o'clock and saw only stars. Eighty-five seconds later – about 19 minutes after midnight – radar told them the target was at 10.00 at 12 miles. The captain saw nothing, but he decided to swing the plane around in a full

69

circle, to get a better look at their left.

At 20-and-a-half minutes after midnight, the captain requested permission to make a left-handed turn. WATCC told him to go ahead and reported simultaneously, "there is another target that has just appeared on your left side about 1 mile... briefly, then disappearing again."

Your Excellencies, what is this behaviour pattern of diving in and out of the Fourth in this rapid, erratic pattern? It does not fit in with Xhemptuwan behaviour and thinking – not even with human mentality, always remembering that humans cannot conceive of the Fourth Dimension, so that these sightings are generally dismissed as human error.

Your Excellencies, the captain then replied, "We haven't got him in sight as yet, but we do pick up the lights around Kaikoura," *Kaikoura* being a Maori word and the name of a stretch of coast.

That is to say, the crew could still see strange lights near the coast from UFOs that *didn't* show on radar.

The plane was now some 66 miles from the radar screen.

The plane banked left, and the radar told them, "The target I mentioned a moment ago is still about 5.00 to you, stationary."

A$_5$ the plane turned, crew and passengers could see all the lights along the coast, the strange lights in the air, but not the object so close to the plane.

At 27 minutes past midnight, the plane had done its full turn, and was flying south again. WATCC called them, "Target is at 12.00 at 3 miles." The captain replied, "Thank you. We pick it up. It's got a flashing light." Later, the captain was to say it had "a couple of very bright blue-white lights, flashing regularly at a rapid rate. They looked like the strobe lights of Boeing 737..."

The cameraman was not getting any shots, because he had to push his camera in front of the face of the co-pilot, who was flying the machine. He tried to pick up some of the Kaikoura lights in his big lens but couldn't, and he didn't want to waste film because the lights were so faint.

But he did some film. He took the take-off from Wellington, which authenticates the film. Then he got an alien blue and white light against the night sky. Then he filmed the instrument panel of the plane, to authenticate further his film. Then he filmed two more alien lights. These he shot for 5, 1.3 and 1.9 seconds. Then the film shows for 5 seconds very indistinct shots of the coastline at Kaikoura with some brighter alien lights in the air above it.

However, Your Excellencies, these brief film shots contravene existing earth science. Nothing inside the cabin could have produced these lights and reflected them on the windshield. They are not planets or stars. They are strong flashes which appeared out of nothing and as such are unacceptable to the human brain.

We have the recorded voice of the reporter, who states, "Now we have a couple right in front of us, very, very bright. That was more an orange-reddy light. It flashed on and then off again... We have a firm convert here at the moment." In the heat of the action, he became an UFO believer.

At 28 minutes after midnight, the Argosy turned to descend into Christchurch. WATCC reported that all targets were 12 to 15 miles behind them.

One minute later, WATWC told them they had an object 1 mile behind them. Four sweeps later, he told them it had dropped back to 4 miles away. Thirty seconds later, he confirmed the 4 miles.

Two sweeps later, he announced in surprise, "There's a strong target right in formation with you. Could be right or left. Your target has doubled in size."

The co-pilot spotted it, and reported, "It was like the fixed navigation lights on a small aircraft when one passes you at night. It was much smaller than the really big ones we had seen over Kaikoura. At irregular intervals it appeared to flash on and off; it brightened or perhaps it twinkled around the edges. When it did this, I could see colour, a slight tinge of green or perhaps red."

The reporter's words were recorded, and he said of it, "I'm looking towards the right of the aircraft and we have an object confirmed by Wellington radar. It's been following us for quite a while. It's about 4 miles away and looks like a very faint star, but then it emits a bright white and green light."

Wellington told the plane that they had gone back to normal size on the screen, and 81 seconds later, the captain told WATCC, "Got a target at 3.00, just behind us," to which the controller replied, "Roger, and going round to 14.00 at 11 miles."

Fifty seconds later, the WATCC controller told Christchurch Air Traffic Control Centre that he had a target at five o'clock at about 10 miles. He said the target was going on and off the screen but "...not moving, not too much speed..." and seconds later, he said, "It is moving in an easterly direction now."

Thirty-five minutes after midnight, WATCC asked the plane, "The target you mentioned, the last one we mentioned, make it 5.00 at 14 miles previously, did you see anything?"

The captain told him, "We saw that one. It came up at four o'clock (not 5.00), I think, around 14 miles away." WATCC replied, "Roger, that target is still stationary. It's now 6.00 to you at about 15 miles and it's been joined by two other targets." The reporter recorded, "That other target that has been following us has been joined by two other targets so at this stage we have three unidentified flying objects just off our right wing and one of them has been probably following us for about 10 minutes."

d)   In France, the *Service d'Expertise de Phenomenes de Rentrees Atmospheriques* has studied about 100 UFO cases.

e)   In Switzerland, in June 1995, six employees of the radar at Dubendorf Military Air Traffic Control saw from their building at Klothen a wide silver disc, wobbling and spinning slowly at 1,700 metres height. Three radar sets registered it.

Your Excellencies, you have entrusted me with an awesome responsibility – to contact the first new planet in 163,000 years.

TV broadcasts from this planet showed UFO activity, and we accepted the interpretation made by unconversant human minds – that the sightings were figments of hysterical imagination, or of other natural atmospheric phenomena.

The UFO sightings did not enter my brief, but, Your Excellencies, I 'sense' a *Cordon Sanitaire* of robot craft out beyond the Oort Cloud. I believe these aliens have found humans dangerous and have wished to quarantine them, that they believe that humans penetrating into space constitute a galactic menace.

I need to study the human brain, and human evolution, and, need much more time to study their behaviour.

I therefore apologise for this very long report, which I believe deals with aliens who are a direct concern to our quadrant. End.

Gulliver had been drinking coffee, and Aldous said, "I'm ready for a bite to eat. Has that coffee spoiled your appetite?"

"Not in the least. Has my report spoiled yours?"

"I don't like those sneaky Little Green Men. Not a bit. I was lucky I didn't get abducted that time. They're not leaving us alone. At least the Shemptoo-ans – I can't pronounce the name of your planet – are heavy-footed, and if cumbersome, at least are full of bonhomie."

"Cumbersome!" snorted Gulliver. "We'd show you a thing or two!"

"Let us to lunch," said Aldous.

* * *

An hour after lunch, the bell rang, and he opened to door to a pretty, buxom twenty-four year old, short blonde hair, a pert nose and an unhappy mouth.

She sat down, showing perfectly formed legs, and said, "I've been engaged now for five long years that seem to have lasted a lifetime. My fiancé is freelancing, writing software, and for four years has been building up his clientele. He's now twenty-eight, but he keeps putting off the wedding. He says he has to get established. I've told him I can help him with my salary, because I'm a secretary. My problem is that he dresses well, is pretty hunky, and I don't know who else he could he getting involved with. Women are attracted to him, not only because he knows how to dress well, but he's got this Mercedes – it's about fourth-hand, but it's a Merce. Why is he putting me off all the time? How is this going to end? He's got his mother and father and a sister, and they all like me, they're all on my side, telling him to make the plunge. I'm getting on in years – I'll soon be twenty-five and I can't wait like this. I'm soon going to be beyond an age that's going to interest guys in marriage."

Aldous smiled. "You'll get married in March next year. Next month, he's going house-hunting with you. You'll find a house after five weeks search, and he'll start paying a mortgage. You'll start putting in bits of furniture, little by little, and by March next year, you'll have just enough furniture to be able to move in after your wedding."

She looked at him radiantly, and opened her handbag, looking for her purse.

* * *

Gulliver came out, and said, "Your human condition is impossible. If she hadn't known about you, she would have thrown that guy over – going by her past experience, which has nothing to do with this fiancé this time. Evolution has gone up a blind track on this planet."

* * *

The next visitor was a scruffy student, tall and thin, with slight beard and moustache that made him look unshaven. He wore a crumpled shirt, a safari-vest and stained shorts, and he peered at Aldous through wire-rimmed spectacles.

He sat down.

"You wouldn't have a cold beer?"

Wordlessly, Aldous fetched him a chilled bottle, with bottle opener.

The student ignored the glass and drank from the neck of the bottle.

"My dad's got a pretty big business and about seventy employees. So, no surprise, he always expected me to go into it. But I'm doing Medicine, and he's so wild he's disinheriting me. I've just finished Third Year – until now, dad hung on in there, because he was hoping I wouldn't hack it. I guess now he's seen there'll be no turning back. Now, when I graduate, it's a bit of a rat race, but I've always been a loner, I always go by what I think, not what they try and tell me –"

He peered at Aldous.

Aldous said, "So you're going to *Doctors Without Frontiers – Medicins Sans Frontiers.*"

The student rocked in his chair, and his jaw fell open.

"They told me you were good, but, man, hey, that's *good.*

"Dad tells me I'll get knocked off – topped by a bullet or if not, a bug'll get me. Let's face it, I'm turning my hack on a lot of hard money, here. Dad's got this fantastic house in Mississauga, so I'm going to have nothing to come back to. I'm going to be cut off. At one stage, the day's going to come when I want to say goodbye to *Doctors Without Frontiers*, look for a hospital appointment, and start saving to buy a roof over my head, here in Toronto. So, there are some sixty-four-dollar ones, sixty-four-dollar questions. Will I get knocked off, what happens when I come back, you know?"

Aldous said, "Your father won't cut you off. When he gets too old, he'll make his firm a shareholding company. He'll sell fifty percent of shares to four managers, who will pay for those shares over 15 years. But seven years after that happens, the firm will go bust, wiped out by new technology. Nothing anybody can do. There'll be no way the firm can adapt to the new technology.

"You'll work for the *Doctors Without Frontiers* for nine years, in Asia and in south America. You'll get enviable experience. Whatever you do, keep a medical diary – each night, detail the cases you have handled that day. That diary will get you into a surgical team in a Toronto Hospital. After another ten years, you'll be earning top fees, and you'll have a big house in Milton."

The student stared a while at Aldous. Then he grinned. "Hey, man, that's great."

He pulled out dollars from his vest, and counted out Aldous' fee.

* * *

Gulliver poked his head around the door. "I've trawled you one you're going to love," he smiled. "Got to keep your spirits up."

She was thirty-three, although disappointed lines made her face older. She obviously did gym and was intelligent, but the last years had sapped her will.

She sat down heavily and said, "I've been married eleven years but we have no children, and children are what I want more than anything else in the world. My husband is infertile, so under medical recommendation, we're going for artificial insemination. Tell me, what will my child be like? I am not allowed to know who the donor is – at least, the Centre where I'm going doesn't tell you."

"He will be excitable and difficult to control..." began Aldous after a pause.

He stopped, and sat in silence for about three minutes.

"You may know that psychics can pass their powers on to their children. Not every copulation results in a psychic child – but we psychics know whether on a particular day we will he fathering a psychic child or not. If we make love now, you will have a psychic child, a girl, with a loving disposition. Do you want me to give you this child?"

She trembled, and stared at him wordlessly, turning very pale.

75

He got up and went to her, putting his hand under her chin. She forced her chin down, staring at the floor. He took her hands and she clenched her fists. Then she looked up at him, frightened.

"This little girl is begging you to let her be born," he said in a low voice, and a shudder went over her body. He pulled on her wrists and she came slackly to her feet as though her muscles had turned to water. He put his arm around her waist and without any resistance from her, he led her to the bedroom, where he slowly undressed her. She put her forehead against his chest, not to look at him.

He laid her naked on the bed, and then stripped, himself. When he lay on top of her, her legs convulsively came together, and with his knee he gently prised them apart. He entered her, and she was very wet. He penetrated her deeply, and she began a low moaning, that grew to a sudden cry as she had an orgasm. She went limp, and Aldous went on. She didn't respond, but lay inert, giving short, sharp cries, that grew louder, and when Aldous poured himself into her, she gave a long cry.

They lay on the bed, while Aldous gently stroked her belly, now flat and firm. It would distend and grow hugely; the thought aroused him and he made love a second time.

Afterwards, lying on the bed, she said, "The other way was impersonal. You've done it much better, but, well – it was a bit personal, wasn't it?"

$$* * *$$

Gulliver brought him a cup of coffee.

"You need this. I've put in plenty of sugar. At least that's one baby who'll have a hope. She'll be able to look after herself, and after other people too. The whole human race should be pursuing children like this – what a hopeless crowd you humans are!"

While they prepared the evening meal, Gulliver said, "Can we fly to London tonight? I have to go to that big library in London. I rang, and got two tickets on a plane leaving at 10pm."

"Jesus!"

"Well, I'm really sorry, but Jesus is really neither here nor there. Is that all right?"

"I'll pack," grumbled Aldous.

"We can sleep on the plane, so we'll arrive at ten in the morning refreshed."

"Don't you count on it," growled Aldous. "People will be getting drunk, making a lot of noise. People who are scared of flying will be talking their heads off all night. We'll have a big cinema screen showing images... God, it's a red-eye flight, you'll see."

"I am here to experience human life in every facet," said Gulliver piously. "It will be one more data."

"Data," said Aldous disgustedly. "What we're going to get is an all-night flight."

Coming out of Heathrow, dazed with lack of sleep and peevish with the west-east jet lag, they took a taxi to Aldous' flat.

In the flat, Gulliver's watch sounded.

GRAND COUNCIL to GULLIVER:

Cruiser squadron despatched to Oort Cloud. Contact with robot Monitors which opened fire, and were inactivated. Full quarantine of solar system. Unknown civilisation, at Ninth Level. End.

"Oh, God," said Aldous exhaustedly. "What now!"

"There are robot ships out there to stop you humans getting out of the solar system and into space. Not that there's any immediate danger. With your trial-and-error science and your chemical fuels and plasma propulsion, you won't be going anywhere. But the Aliens in this other quadrant – well, fact is, they don't like you. Not one little bit. And they're a hundred thousand years ahead of you."

"What's this of the Ninth Level?"

"My Confederation is at the Fifteenth Level. You are at Level One, and I have come here to see whether we can take you on three thousand years into the Second Level of science and technology."

"In these circumstances, I think the best course we can follow is go to bed, and catch up with some sleep."

"Excellent idea, brother dear," said Gulliver soothingly.

* * *

At three o'clock, Aldous had a shower, and went downstairs to do some shopping. On the stairs, he ran into his downstairs neighbour, the lawyer.

"Ernest," exclaimed Aldous. It's good to see you."

Ernest was a successful barrister, stocky, curly hair and a chubby face

78

that looked younger than his forty-five years. He had deceptively innocent blue eyes and a deceptive smile."

"Aldous!" he said. "I've been ringing your bell for two days. We're flying up to Aberdeen in about an hour's time to take my boat across to Oslo. Would you care to come with us?"

"Truth to tell, I'm not alone. A long-lost brother has found me – a half brother I never knew existed, and who's my spitting image – well, almost. A very strong likeness."

"Consider him invited."

"Ernest, we've just got in from Canada."

"Think about it. We leave tomorrow about eleven in the morning.

He pulled out his notebook, and wrote quickly.

"Here's where we're moored. Well, I've got to get out to Heathrow. I do hope you both can make it, old chap."

Ernest's yacht was fifty-five feet long, and had cabin accommodation for ten.

* * *

Aldous came back with his shopping, and found Gulliver awake. They cooked and had something to eat; then walked around London, Aldous showing Gulliver the city.

Back at the flat, in the living-room, Aldous stopped dead. "That yacht of Ernest's, *The Golden Fleece*! Something's going to happen. The... the... rudder?"

After several moments, Gulliver nodded. "A summer storm, a gale – oh, dear! Can you phone him?"

"I've got his mobile phone. But he would never listen."

"Ring him."

Ernest answered.

"Aldous here. Don't make this trip in your boat. You're going to hit a storm and lose your rudder."

"We'll call the Lifeboat Service," laughed Ernest. "Aldous, please!"

"The yacht will broach before the Lifeboat arrives."

"Sounds like a lot of excitement," drawled Ernest. "Aldous, please, do come. You can warn us in time. But don't worry. She's a big boat and summer blows are never that bad. I'll he expecting you. You can't let us get lost with all hands! See you!"

Ernest broke the connection.

* * *

Next morning, Aldous awoke in deep unease.

They made breakfast, washed the dishes, and went back to the living-room.

Gulliver announced calmly, "Oh dear, I do fear that we have unwelcome visitors."

Aldous concentrated, and sweat broke out on his face.

"It's a tax man. From Internal Revenue. He's going to pose as someone wanting a Reading. He's carrying marked banknotes. There are two detectives with him, who will follow him in when he lays the banknotes down somewhere. He's not going to bother with the Reading. He'll just plant the banknotes on me!"

Gulliver chided him, "When you have so much money, why do you try to cheat the Government of these miserable sums — why don't you pay your taxes like everyone else?"

"Because they're all thieves, and it's a rip-off."

"An anarchist," Gulliver reproved him. "What a mess. Well, we'll have to fix this." He smiled broadly.

"There, that's that!"

Aldous looked at him in fright.

"That's what?" he cried.

Gulliver said smugly, "The three of them are now in the main street of the capital of Bermuda."

"*What!*" whispered Aldous. "Oh, no!" he wailed.

"When the uninstructed cross my path, I have an obligation to educate them," said Gulliver, with satisfaction.

"They're the Law!"

"Some Law! They won't do any more harm."

Aldous said urgently, "They'll find a Police Station. They'll identify themselves. They'll phone Scotland Yard. This flat will be surrounded by the Army, the Navy and the Airforce. There'll be SAS at all the windows."

"All right," said Gulliver calmly. "Repack your things. Make the bed. Get all your money, and leave the door of your safe ajar. I'll pack, and clear away the breakfast things."

Fifteen minutes, Gulliver said, "Bring your suitcases here. That's right. Now stand exactly here."

Aldous was swept into swirling lights and racing tendrils of grey and red.

Then he was standing beside a shed on a pier. Gulliver said proudly, "Aberdeen. There's The Golden Fleece. It's only ten-thirty, and Ernest said he would sail at eleven. Let's carry our luggage on board."

Aldous was shaking.

What were all those lights?" he asked in a strangled voice.

"The Fourth Dimension. Of course, you haven't been there before. Not to worry. It's all behind you. Now we must needs go down to the sea, down to the wild sea and the waves. I'm ever so pleased I drew this assignment."

They took their luggage up the gangway, calling out for Ernest, who looked over a railing on an upper deck.

"Aldous! Good man! I knew you wouldn't abandon me without a rudder!"

He vanished, then appeared in a doorway on their deck.

He went up to Gulliver and shook hands.

"The likeness is amazing. You must tell me the whole story. Is this really the first time you two have met? Four decades or something like that?"

Aldous introduced them.

Ernest said, "Gulliver, welcome on board. Let me show you your cabins, and get this luggage out of the way. Are either of you bad sailors, because you'll need to take seasickness tablets this very minute? They take a while to work."

Aldous grinned, and nodded. "I think we're going to need them."

Ernest led them into a large lounge, and on to a passage-way at the far end. He opened one of the doors, and showed them a two-bunk cabin.

"Make yourselves at home. I'm going to get those seasickness pills."

He came back in a couple of minutes, and handed them the pills. They took water from the tap above a basin. Ernest made himself comfortable in a chair, while they unpacked. Aldous told him the whole story of Gulliver being a half-brother, and how they had met by sheer chance at Pickle Creek.

Then Ernest led them up to the bridge, and introduced them to the Captain.

Ernest said, "I'm a sort of First Mate. I've got Certificates, but I'm happier with John on board."

John said, "I'm a Charter Captain, but if Ernest advises me well enough in advance, I try to help him out."

Aldous probed gently. Ernest did pay John, and well.

Ernest laughed. "John's the pro here... Aldous and Gulliver were in

81

Canada. Just got back."

John was busy, hut kept up a running conversation about Canada and about canoeing.

He started the engine, and two men below cast off the ropes.

Ernest led them down into the lounge, and introduced them to two married couples. They went into the galley and made themselves tea, and sat on the sofas talking.

Gulliver said, "Aldous has a thing about taxes," and one of the other men, heavily jowled, laughed and said, "Don't we all! I've got an engineering business, and I wish I could move it to a tax haven somewhere."

They got into an involved conversation about tax rates, tax rebates and tax loopholes.

* * *

After lunch, they sat talking. The wives were about forty, snobs, with distinguished faces, marked by the years. They talked about London parties and gossiped. Gulliver listened, enthralled. They named politicians and public figures. Then, casually, they chatted up Gulliver. He told them he had been a geologist, prospecting in lonely parts of Australia, and they treated him with hauteur. He went on to tell them about gems, their value, the markets, how to cut them... he had their rapt attention. When they suggested Bridge, he joined them, with a husband making up the foursome.

At four o'clock, a moderate gale had blown up. Aldous and Ernest went out on deck, with the wind blowing keenly. The wind rose to a fresh gale, and the ship was rolling. At five o'clock, the wind rose to a strong gale, and Ernest led Aldous inside, and showed him how to wind down steel shutters, protecting the lounge windows.

Ernest explained, "We should really call this a saloon, but depending who you invite on hoard, they find the word an incredibly vulgar Americanism, which is entirely wrong, and shows a poor grasp of the language."

Aldous went with Ernest along the passageway, and into each of the cabins, where they lowered more steel screens over the windows.

By 5.20, it was blowing a whole gale and the ship began plunging and rolling hard. Back in the lounge, the two married couples could not hide their worry.

"These summer storms," muttered one of the husbands.

Ernest said, "Aldous can tell the future. Ask him whether we'll be all right."

The ladies laid down their cards, and plied him with questions. He answered patiently, and they almost forgot the weather.

At 5.45, it was blowing a storm, and at six, a hurricane. The sound of the engines dropped away to a murmur, and Aldous went with Ernest to the bridge.

John said, "I've throttled back just to keep on steering way. We've turned north, and we'll have to run before it. We've got a wind-controlled automatic helmsman, to keep her from broaching. We're being pushed along about seven knots."

It was gusting eighty miles an hour. The skies were black, and rain drove out of the racing, low clouds. Thirty-foot waves overtook the yacht, reared high above it, then swept over the stern and along its length, to cover the bows, and blur the wheelhouse windows with pouring water.

The bridge had all-around armoured windows, so they could see the waves climb up behind, overtake them and pour along the length of the ship.

The yacht rose effortlessly out of the tons of water, raised its bows and rode up each wave before it slipped away, and the bows plunged into a valley of black, dark-green, reddish-hued water, where horizontal lines of spume writhed and twisted across the sudden wall of sea before it.

"Listen," said Ernest. "You've got jet-lag, and right now would have been your Canadian bedtime. Would you care to turn in, while I stand watch with John till about midnight? I wake you up, and you can stand watch — what say you?"

"Good idea!"

They went down to the cabin, and Gulliver came with them. The bunk had high, polished, wooden sides, but Ernest took straps out of a drawer, and showed them how to secure them.

They stripped to their underwear, climbed over the high side of the bunk, and secured the straps to hold them in.

Stretched out on the mattress, the movement of The Golden Fleece felt wilder, but they fell asleep.

Ernest woke them at midnight. They dressed, went to the galley to eat, and have coffee. The careening of the yacht made eating a balancing act; then they went up to the bridge.

John smiled at them haggardly.

"The automatic-steering puts us on a bearing of about 330°, but I want to make for Wick. So I've disconnected the automatic, and am steering on 314°. If we get too much sea offside, I put on the automatic and let her bear up to wherever the wind wants to take her. I don't know how well you follow that, but I don't know how to explain it in layman's terms. If *I'm* doing the steering and she starts rolling too heavily, I've got to let her straighten up with the automatic so we've got the seas behind us again, and not on our side."

Aldous said, "That's pretty clear. Would you like us to steer?"

John gave him the wheel.

"Watch the compass. When she goes off 314°, correct immediately, and when she swings back, straighten the wheel before she reaches 314°."

Aldous steered for thirty minutes, with John watching him, and correcting him.

Then John went to a high-backed chair, strapped himself in, and rested. In a few minutes he was asleep.

Aldous said to Gulliver, "The rudder's going to break at nine o'clock this morning. We'll have to call the Lifeboat at seven."

Gulliver nodded. "We'll wake Ernest at half-past-six."

From one o'clock until three, they held the course at 314°, but then the yacht was staggering and rolling under the smashing impact of the waves, the decks running white; they ran before the storm at 005° degrees, heading at a slight angle away from Wick.

At half-past-four, they tried to ease back to 330°, but she rolled so badly her gunwales went under.

At half-past-five, they woke John, who went down for coffee and sandwiches.

He came back, took the wheel, and said, "We're coming up to the entry of Pentland Firth but we're not going to make Wick. We're going to be carried up west of the Orkneys."

At half-past-six, they woke up Ernest. They went with him to the galley, and while he drank coffee and ate with one hand, holding on with the other, Aldous said, "You have to radio for the lifeboat at 6.58 exactly. We will see the lifeboat at 9.03, and the rudder will go at 9.01."

Ernest's face was agonised.

"I *can't* radio if the rudder's okay. Suppose it *doesn't* break!"

"It will break, the boat will broach, turn turtle, and everyone will drown," grated Aldous.

Gulliver nodded. "Everyone will drown."

Ernest said, "Now you're going to tell me that Gulliver has this gift too."

"In a minor way," said Gulliver modestly. "But, my goodness, how it works when there's danger. And now it's screaming at me. Six fifty-eight. We've got five minutes."

"Come on," said Ernest, and they went to the radio shack, and put out the call.

In the early daylight, the sea terrified them.

The Golden Fleece rolled and pitched, driven north at some seven knots.

At half-past-eight, a cross-sea built up, with violent changes in the wind.

The yacht yawed and pitched like a maddened thing, the waves running at right angles to each other. Her speed dropped off from seven knots to five, then two. The hurricane mounted with a savagery that chilled their blood. In the ferocity of the Force 12 sea, the stanchions of her rails were smashed and rails swept overboard.

At one minute to nine, the rudder went, and John stared at them with a frozen face.

Two minutes later, they saw the lifeboat, and John watched it with unbelieving eyes.

The yacht was halfway broached to, when they saw a crew member of the lifeboat standing in the bows, fifteen feet above them, with a line.

John went out onto the deck, clipped onto the lifeline.

The sea was like a boiling cauldron. The seas were crashing into each other, sideways, so that they 'compressed' the water and sent it flying crazily skyward.

The yacht reared up on a mountainous wave, and they looked far down below at the lifeboat and crew member in the bows.

The Golden Fleece descended sickeningly, and the lifeboat reared up high into the spray, and fired the line. John got it, and secured it. Then he reeled it in, to bring a heavier tow onto the yacht, and in the midst of an appalling fury of water, he attached it.

The lifeboat began its tow, the yacht sheering now madly to port, now starboard, and after forty minutes, the line began to strand.

A second lifeboat appeared. They got on a tow astern, and the second lifeboat held them steady.

On the radio, Ernest asked, "Where's the best place to fix the rudder?"

and the lifeboat coxwain told them, "Scrabster. I'll take you to Scrabster, if you like."

They were in Scrabster before eleven o'clock.

They took rooms at the hotel, and Ernest and his engineer passenger went to see about repairs to the rudder.

After lunch, the party went into Thurso, and walked around the town, the ladies leading them into shops. They went to a pub, and one of the wives said, "What an awful night. Sleeping strapped into the bank. Despite all the heaving around, it is really astonishing but one does sleep, you know."

She smiled at Aldous. "How did you sleep?"

"We went up on the bridge to watch the waves."

* * *

Back in Scrabster for their evening meal, Aldous asked, "Weren't you surprised at John going to sleep like that?"

"I confess I put him to sleep. I could see that you were dying to play at wee boats."

"Those waves frightened the life out of me."

"They didn't frighten the life out of Ernest. He was unflappable. Is he slightly mad? Who would want to own a yacht?"

"Ernest is a barrister, and he *is* unflappable, which helps him no end in Court. He needs the yacht to relax, to relieve him of his stress."

"STRESS! And what was last night?"

"Ernest is really uncomplicated, but the complexities of human behaviour defy all description. He loves showing off his vessel, having guests on board – he loves conversation, he loves the sea."

"Loves the SEA!"

"Well," said Aldous dubiously. "He does. He's a womaniser but he never takes his girlfriends on board. He prefers groups of friends, to socialise and talk."

"And hopefully to drown them," muttered Gulliver.

Next day, they took the Scrabster ferry to Stromness. All night, the wind had battered the windows of the hotel, but after breakfast, it had died away. The ferry sailed through a calm sea of long, glassy swells. Gulliver gazed at The Old Man of Hoy, a high-stacked tower of dark rock, and said, "That makes me think of Xhemptuw."

"Homesick?" asked Aldous.

"We don't have those emotions – but inside a human body, I can feel your human emotions stirring up there," and he pointed to his head, and smiled.

At Stromness, they paid for a bus tour, and the bus carried them to Maes Howe, a high, man-made symmetrical hill, covered with grass, in the middle of flat country.

They were led to the hill, where they had to crouch to enter a low stone tunnel. Aldous went along it on all-fours; the tunnel went on and on, trying his patience. Then he entered a chamber lit by electric light bulbs, and thankfully stood up.

He found himself inside a Stone Age Cathedral. Drystone slabs of rocks, uncemented, soared far above his head to a height that staggered him. He stared up for two or three minutes, trying to comprehend what he was seeing.

He lowered his glance. He stood in a circular chamber, with straight walls, all of drystone rock without cement. Into the walls were openings the size of doorways, and stepping to one, he looked in and saw around the corner a stone platform.

"They laid the dead there, till they decomposed, and then took the bones for burial. They may have needed the bones to ensure that land stayed in the family. They could have served as Title Deeds."

"A charnel house," said Ernest, disapprovingly. "And what soaring beauty."

"Ernest, you are eloquent this morning," said one of the wives. She asked the guide, "Do you suppose they blocked up the opening for a couple of years. The odour – imagine!"

The guide said, "We just don't know. It's so many thousands of years ago. They would have used clay or earth, and that leaves no traces."

He showed runes scratched in a slab.

"These were Vikings who wintered here, a couple of thousand years ago, or more perhaps. This was already ancient when the Vikings came."

Outside, the engineer said, "How we've advanced when you think of it. Look at us today. Incredible!"

Gulliver smiled quizzically at Aldous, and sent, "Oh yeah!"

The bus drove them to Skara Brae, a Stone Age village more recent than Maes Howe, but thousands of years old.

It stood in the sand dunes, close to the beach. They entered a drystone, circular cattle pen, through an outer opening that could be closed at night with a great slab of rock.

On the opposite side, another opening led to a passageway, like the passage in a hotel with rooms on each side.

An enormous slab closed the way into the passage, with its beehive homes of drystone, uncemented stone. Each dwelling had a low entrance, with a stone lintel, and another slab to shut off the doorway. Around the walls inside stood slabs to contain grass for bedding. Stone stools in the middle stood around a hearth; and gaps in the stone walls served as shelves and cupboards.

The dwellings touched each other, presenting an unbroken wall to the world outside, and the passage had probably been covered.

The guide said, "One night a terrific storm drove them out. They escaped so fast that we found a necklace on the ground in a doorway. The storm covered the village with sand, and it lay hidden thousands of years, till a great storm in 1850."

Gulliver climbed above it to the side, and stood rooted, looking at it for fifteen minutes.

They called them back to the buses.

* * *

The bus drove them around Scapa Flow, and the guide told them how the First World War German Fleet lay scuppered on the bottom. Gulliver's face was stone.

In Kirkwall, they went to the cathedral, and saw a young Austrian, dressed in leather shorts with straps over his shoulders, up in the organ loft, playing Bach.

Gulliver said, grimly, "They had to scuttle the German Fleet outside before they could learn to let young Austrians come here and play Bach."

They went outside and walked around Kirkwall.

Gulliver said, "After the storm yesterday, and now after this abandoned Stone Age village, I finally understand everything that has happened on this planet."

Aldous said, with ironic asperity, "Remarkable."

Gulliver said, "This planet is savage – was savage, and still is. I saw that sea yesterday. Evolution went up blind lanes – got lost in its task. It had one commitment only – *to survive*. As fast as it found solutions, they were wiped out. All that mattered was to find new solutions. Peopling the planet with predators, evolution made it far worse. Evolution was not concerned with higher forms of consciousness such as are found on our planets. Consciousness served only to survive and propagate genes. Those Stone Age people at Scara Brae built themselves what? – a defensive fortress. Enemies did not drive them out. The planet did. The natural, primeval behaviour of the planet did that."

On the ferry back to Scrabster, Aldous worried, "I wonder whether they've tried to force an entry to my flat in London?"

"They didn't force an entry. An electronic expert deciphered the code of your lock, and opened your door easily."

"My God, suppose they plant marked money or whatever?"

"Two men entered ahead and vanished. One of the other three tossed in a coin, and that vanished. They decided to close the door and go back to Scotland Yard."

"Oh, Jesus," moaned Aldous in misery. "You sent them to Hamilton."

"No, they went to Anchorage in Alaska. And a much better trip they had of it than ourselves, in that yacht, The Golden Fleece. You can envy them, indeed you can. A holiday abroad never hurt anyone," Gulliver added virtuously. "Return fare paid for by the taxpayer."

Aldous said desperately, "I'm going to be grilled for a year."

"Calm down, probe into the future, you'll see you'll be all right. Relax, and use your psychic powers."

"My psychic powers don't work very well for myself – a most peculiar thing. I get warnings, deep unease, but not the details I get with other people."

Gulliver said comfortably, "Just forget the matter and think how those policemen in Anchorage didn't get the fright they did in Bermuda. They were forewarned. One of them had even put his toothbrush in his pocket."

They docked at Oslo, and went ashore.

Gulliver told Aldous, "I won't come with you to Gothenburg. I'd like a couple of weeks wandering around on my own. I might go down to Denmark and Germany. We'll meet up at Gothenburg airport."

"How! I don't know what flight I'll be catching to Spain, or on what day."

Gulliver grinned. "Just you buy your ticket, take your decision, and I'll read your mind."

"But you're going off on your own..."

"Just a little look around."

He landed in Gothenburg in mid-afternoon, and Maj-Britt was at Landvetter to meet him. She ran to his arms, and kissed him with passion, then took his arm and led him out to the car.

"Have you missed me?"

Aldous said, "You can't begin to imagine."

"All those other women you must have," she teased him.

"You're the only person in the whole world," he said, stopping, his hands holding luggage, leaning forward to press his cheek against hers.

"Ah, if I can believe it," she said, laughing.

"It's true," he swore.

At the car, she unlocked the doors, and he pushed the luggage in the back seat, then got in beside her as she took the wheel.

"Three long weeks," signed Maj-Britt.

"Much worse for me," he avowed.

She wove into the traffic.

"How are the girls?"

"Annika's suffering love pangs, and Lena gets very intense about other people's troubles. Do you suppose that's normal at thirteen?"

"When a girl's psychic, nothing's normal, I imagine," he said heavily. "This sounds interesting. Well, apart from that, everything's all right?"

Maj-Britt said carefully, "We-e-ll, there's been a lot of expenses. I've overrun by about ten thousand crowns –"

"What!" he cried, swinging around sharply to stare at her.

"You've got no idea what everything costs to run –"

"Especially when you never keep any accounts. I give you thirty thousand crowns a month for the three of you, and there's no rent to pay!"

He probed sharply. She still had her two lovers, Kalle, the twenty-one-year-old student in his student cap with the white top, an oversexed stud... no... no, no AIDS... and the factory manager, Bo, some sort of nickname... no AIDS... so-so in bed, but he took her out in the evenings, restaurants, concerts –

He probed harder. Ten thousand crowns!

God in heaven! She'd given it to the young prick of a Kalle to help furnish his new flat.

92

All the air was knocked out of him.

He breathed slowly and deeply several times.

"Maj-Britt, listen to me," he said with a steady deliberateness. "I know all about young Kalle..."

She swerved so hard she almost collided.

"Slow down," he commanded.

"I also know you've given him that ten thousand. So for the next five months, I'll give you 28,000 crowns a month, till I recover the ten thousand."

She argued feebly, "Who is Kalle? How can we live on twenty-eight thousand a month?"

"Listen," he said, reasonably. "I admire you Swedes for your sexual freedom and your casual attitude to sex, and I don't begrudge you your excitements. I have joined my life to yours because of your nympho streak, and we have had two wonderful girls. I'm sure Kalle gives you wonderful orgasms, but *keep my money out of it*," he warned her, in a rising voice.

"I haven't given a penny to anyone," she said weakly. "And didn't you once say you drew more than a million crowns a year from your business. You give me only a quarter of that..."

"Have you any idea, the remotest idea, of the expenses I have in this Portfolio Management business, travelling all the time between Torre Real, Jersey, London and Toronto?"

"You've got one brother in Toronto, another in Jersey and another in Torre Real, all three running your offices. But there's no one in London."

"I keep telling, you I do psychic consultations in London. Please don't let us argue. Twenty-eight thousand crowns, and if you want to break up our relationship –"

"No!" she shrieked, and the car swerved again. She began to weep.

"Do you want me to drive?" he asked urgently. "You're going to have an accident."

"I am all right," she sniffed.

Twenty minutes later, she turned into Aschebergsgatan, slowed down in front of a venerable stone-built building of distinction, and drove down an underground ramp.

They took the lift from the garage, and gazing at her, Aldous felt desire stir strongly. She wore a simple, expensively-cut black dress, low over her small hard breasts, thin straps over her shoulders. She was thirty-seven, with long blonde hair, and looked twenty-eight, despite the vaguely sad mouth often found in Swedish women. Her eyes were blue, large and expressive, exotically slanted above full cheekbones, and held a hint of sexual mockery that aroused him uncomfortably. He didn't want to greet his daughters with an erection, so he looked at the roof of the lift and forced his thoughts hurriedly onto the Dow Jones Index.

93

Was Gulliver a psychic hallucination?

When Maj-Britt unlocked the front door, his daughters ran down the passage and flung their arms around him.

His younger daughter, Lena, thirteen-years-old, cried, "You've been away three weeks. You're cruel!"

He struggled along the passageway, with his daughters and his luggage.

It was an old-fashioned flat, the living-room wide, the ceiling very high, with plaster bas-reliefs of cornucopiae touched in gold and red and green. The furniture was incongruously modern Scandinavian, of golden wood in flowing lines and lemon-tinted upholstery.

Aldous dropped his luggage and tried to embrace both girls at once.

They were tall, thin, with shoulder-length blonde hair, and beautiful.

Lena wept, "I'm so unhappy and when I need you you're not here."

Aldous turned to Annika. "Are you unhappy too?"

"My life is in ruins." She checked a sob.

"Then I'm going straight back to the airport," said Aldous, going to pick up his luggage.

Both girls jumped on him.

"You beast," laughed his wife.

The girls pushed him to the sofa, and Lena sat on his lap, so he couldn't get up, and Annika hung on to his arm.

Aldous sighed. "Lena. Tell me. I'm listening."

"You told me I can never, never let anyone know that I'm psychic."

"And now I tell you yet one time more, Lena. Young people don't tolerate those who are very different. You have to study and then go to

University. When you grow up, you'll have a whole lifetime to proclaim to the world at large whatever you care to. At your age, if your peers find out about you your life will become an unexampled misery."

"Daddy," Lena wailed, "All sorts of awful things are going on. Scores of things. This girl at school... her mother's going to get cancer and it won't be diagnosed in time and she's going to die in awful pain. I can't live with myself. A boy I know is going to be killed by a car within two weeks."

Aldous said severely, "Life is an ocean of desperate suffering. What you're talking about is the merest of mere drops in that ocean. You have a huge responsibility to yourself. One day you can help right these wrongs, hut now your responsibility –"

He looked at her unblinkingly.

"YOUR RESPONSIBILITY," he said menacingly, "is to get through school and University."

Annika said, "Daddy, you don't know what it's like. The same thing happens to me, although now I can live with it, but I don't know how. Daddy, how can people live without knowing what's going to happen. How can they!"

Aldous said, "What's for tea, Maj-Britt? It is just possible that you girls are unaware that your mother's a *cordon bleu* chef."

The girls jumped up and put their arms around their mother.

"We do! We do!"

"No one can do raw fish in vinegar like her," said Aldous smacking his lips.

"If you don't watch your tongue, that's what you're going to get," she warned him.

"What's on the menu?" he pleaded in humility.

"Fish and potato-chip pie, covered with thick grated cheese. That followed by redberry pie."

"My waistline," he groaned.

"It will fill you with energy," she said, with wicked suggestion.

He thought about the coming night in bed with her

He smiled beatifically at his family.

"You two!" expostulated Annika.

Aldous gave a guilty start. He had forgotten they were psychic.

"Concupiscence," mocked Lena.

Maj-Britt didn't even blush. "You two girls stop it. Your turn will come quickly enough. Men can't help themselves," and at that Aldous roared at her, "Men can't help being instinctive poets."

Annika sat down beside him. "Daddy" she said sadly, "My life is in ruins. You must help me."

"Go on, darling. I'm listening."

"His name is Bernt. He's the best-looking boy in the school, and although he doesn't know it, I can see his future, and he's going to be a famous film star. We had long, long talks. Our conversations were so sensitive and understanding. He made me feel our spirits were touching. He made me feel I was finding myself with his tenderness."

"Extraordinary," murmured Aldous.

"And then this hussie –"

Annika broke into tears.

"She's got the most vulgar body in the whole class. Disgusting buttocks, great big floppy boobs." She sobbed. "She opened her legs, and now Bernt hasn't got another thought in his head but her vulva –"

"There, there," said Aldous, nonplussed at this Swedish openness with sex.

"Daddy, what can I do!"

"Thank God, that's easy to answer."

"Yes," she cried eagerly.

"Find another chap."

"Oh, daddy," she stormed. "That's impossible."

"Another chap," he said sternly.

"Oh, you men are so unfeeling!" she said in despair.

"The whole problem is that you girls are urban dwellers and cut off from life in the countryside and down on the farm."

His daughters looked at him suspiciously.

"When you put a bull to a cow, after about three times, it loses interest. But you change the cow and you'll see what enthusiasm."

"And what else?" said Annika narrowly.

"If a cow has been serviced, and you bring a new bull –"

"I'm going to scratch your eyes out," said Annika. "I'm going to cut out your tongue –"

"Don't you love your poor old feeble dad any more, darling?" he said with pathos.

"Mummy," howled Lena, "He's calling us 'cows'. Mummy!"

"Stop teasing those silly girls," said Maj-Britt.

* * *

Annika said sulkily, "As you won't take me seriously and won't help me –"

"I've just given you the best advice you've ever heard and in fifty years time –"

"Fifty years! Fifty years doesn't exist! But I need your help for something else. My best friend is Ulla, she'll soon be sixteen... and she's going to have a baby."

"Oooh!" said Lena.

"She wants to commit suicide, because the father is only sixteen and at school. But I told her you would advise her and save her as soon as you arrived."

"Annika!" he expostulated, in exasperated incredulity. "Forget it!"

"We have an hour before supper is ready, and Ulla is expecting us now. When I saw you arriving in the car I gave her a quick ring."

"No," he said, "No, and no."

"Let me explain everything as we are walking along. I don't dare tell her I'm psychic –"

"I should think not –"

"So I'll explain to you what I have found, and you can pretend it's come from you."

"No," he said. "No, and no."

"I've probed, and found a couple in Italy who want to adopt. If they take her, she will become an Art Critic; love her adopted parents and Ulla too, her real parent; and form a happy family. She'll work from her house as a Critic, so she'll make a real home for her children."

Aldous transfixed her with his look.

Then slowly he got to his feet.

"Do you have the names and address?" he challenged.

She took a paper from her pocket.

He studied it in silence.

Then, after a long pause, he memorised it.

* * *

Outside, they walked down Aschebergsgatan to Vasa Gatan, which they followed to Haga Nygata and on to Fjärde Långgatan, and turned up a side street.

Annika rang the Interphone, and they were buzzed in.

On the second floor, the door to the flat was open, and a harassed lady ushered them in, speaking Swedish.

"She says how welcome you are, and thanks you for coming."

She led them into a small room with chairs, and Ulla stood waiting for them.

Ulla glanced nervously at Aldous, then looked down at the floor, and took Annika's hand. The girls sat on a settee, Aldous in a chair.

Ulla's shoulders twitched, while she looked at the floor, then glanced distraught at Annika.

She sneaked another look at Aldous.

Aldous said, "You don't have to give your baby to the social workers. You can give your baby for adoption."

Ulla looked at him wordlessly, with a small hope growing in her face.

"As you know, I'm psychic. If you have the baby here, it will be registered and it'll take a couple of years to arrange adoption. If you are in contact with your child from the beginning, afterwards you won't want to give it up. It s better it be born abroad in a country where they aren't so bureaucratic as Sweden, where you can give it to the doting parents immediately, and they find a wet-nurse, or a nurse who knows what sort of feed-bottles to give to a newborn baby. Now I'm going to think."

He sat there.

"A couple in England want to adopt. Your daughter –"

Ulla made an exclamation.

"Your daughter will be a bad student, and will grow up uncontrollable. No.

"I have a couple in – in – New Zealand. Your daughter will be a bad student but will become a housewife. No! No! You'll have trouble at Auckland Airport, trying to get out of the country."

He sat quietly.

"I have another couple in Germany who are desperately anxious – no – no – wait, wait, there is a couple in Italy. Your girl will be a bad student, but she will be intensely interested in art. She will become an Art Critic, stay in touch with you, look after you when you get old... do you want to go Italy to have your baby?"

Ulla nodded dumbly, and Annika called in her mother.

Annika explained in Swedish while Aldous wrote down the name and address.

He said, "You must get the phone number from the Gothenburg Telephone Exchange. This Italian couple speak English. You must explain that you will go to Italy to have the baby. After you have the baby, you will cross into France by rail, and catch a plane at Marseilles to return to Gothenburg. You will live with this couple for three months, and you will become firm friends, lifelong friends. They are wealthy, and very nice."

He sat back, his face covered in perspiration.

* * *

Out in the street, Annika said, "You must be annoyed you are not getting one thousand five hundred crowns. How *can* you charge people when you have so much money?"

"Because then they take it very seriously. Annika, you were extraordinary. I just couldn't 'find' those people. And then I did. I was afraid you may have made a mistake. You are extraordinary, my child."

Annika protested, "Not only do you charge, but you evade taxes."

"Do you realise your mother gets thirty thousand crowns a month. Ten thousand is by cheque, which pays a tiny tax. The other twenty thousand, I give her in cash, so it's tax free. To the point that she receives help from the Swedish government, being in a low-income group at ten thousand."

"Why do you rob the government, how can you?"

"Because politicians are thieves. In Europe, they take sixpence in every ten and only give back about tuppence, in pensions and so on. The politicians are black holes – they suck in our freedom and give out nothing in return."

"You can't steal people's freedom in Europe. It's democratic."

"When you steal sixpence in tenpence, you are stealing more than half of people's freedom, because money is freedom. Democracy was to replace ancient tyrannies but today politicians have autocratic powers that ancient despots never dreamed of."

"When Ulla gets back to Gothenburg, Social Services will be on to her. How is she going to explain away that she doesn't have her baby with her?"

"Tell her that in the Italian Hospital, they will bring her a lot of papers to fill out and sign. That's for the Italian Civil Registry. They will give her copies, to take to the Swedish Consulate, to register her baby as a Swede. Tell her not to go anywhere near her Consulate. Bring all the papers back with her to Gothenburg, and keep them very carefully. The people from the Italian Hospital won't go to the Swedish Consulate, because they'll be quite sure that Ulla will go, and until the Italian Registry notifies the Swedish Consulate – I imagine that will be never."

At home, they sat in the living-room, waiting for Maj-Britt to call them.

Annika glanced at Lena, then said diffidently, "We are both getting images of an awful lot of half-brothers and half-sisters out there."

Aldous swallowed nervously.

"Have you seen how ordinary people have to live without knowing what's going to happen?"

Lena shuddered.

"So the more psychics, the better, I should say."

"Aaah," said both girls in unison.

"Now suppose both of you both have twenty children who are psychic

– you use contraceptives until you know that on that particular night you're going to have a psychic baby, and then that night you take no precautions so it can happen."

"Ugh!" said Lena. "We have learnt at school that it has taken thousands of years to reach the freedom women enjoy now."

"Maybe all those children would love you like mad."

The girls' expressions grew misty.

"So you're helping mankind," said Annika, ironically.

"I think you're an important help to mankind, Annika."

"Oh, well, I'm different."

"I'm an important help to mankind," said Lena complacently, "but you won't let me help."

"Suppose you had forty children, and then those children each had twenty kids. In a few generations..."

"Daddy, you're being sweet and unselfish," said Annika evenly. "But I'd like to meet some of my brothers and sisters ... '

"I'm going crazy with curiosity," complained Lena. Aldous began to perspire, when Maj-Britt called them, and he jumped to his feet and hurried into the dining-room. Before he sat down, he turned to his daughters, and whispered fiercely, "Not a word to your mother!"

They meekly nodded.

What the devil was Gulliver doing?

Over the meal, Aldous asked them, "Would you like to go up to the house in Amäs tomorrow?"

The girls shouted, "Oh, daddy, yes!" but Maj-Britt said, "We've got to get on the plane first."

"I booked six weeks ago, and I've got the tickets in my briefcase. If we're not going to use them, I'll have to ring now to get the money back."

Maj-Britt stared at him. "You're astonishing. Why didn't you say anything?"

"I had to be sure that business wouldn't tie me up."

"How long can we go for?" Lena asked.

"We can take out the boat for a week, then I've got to come back. I've got a ticket booked. But I've booked you three back at the end of August."

The girls were elated, and Maj-Britt looked at him with sparkling eyes.

"We'll pack tonight. What time does the plane leave?"

"At two. About 50 minutes to Stockholm, then another 55 minutes flight to Umeå. About two hours on the bus."

They were grinning at each other.

Afterwards, Aldous asked, "Has anyone rung asking for readings?"

"I've got three phone numbers," said Maj-Britt. "They wanted to know when you'd be in Gothenburg."

"I'll ring them now and see whether they can come tomorrow morning."

"Mmm," said Annika. "Three times one thousand five hundred crowns... now, what would that come to?"

* * *

In bed that night, Maj-Britt said, "Let's see whether you still have that voracious sexual appetite."

"I always remember I'm a gentleman."

"Don't you dare," she said.

The first visitor next morning came at quarter-to-ten. He was forty, very well dressed, with a firm, concentrated expression, a quirk of humour on his lips, and he said in a businesslike way, "I've got to fly to Peru, and do some flying

101

in small planes up into the lower Andes, or some mountains or the other, whatever they're called. I won't conceal it, I'm scared stiff."

"Not to worry," said Aldous. "You will be perfectly safe."

"Now a second question..."

Aldous smiled. "No, you're not going to catch some disease no one has ever heard of."

The man started, then looked at Aldous, impressed, and shook his head.

"You'll come back safe and sound. But in April next year, you will be sent to the United States. You will have to take feeder flights on twelve and fourteen-seater planes. Don't get on any of those planes. One of them will crash, killing everyone except the pilot. If necessary, talk to your doctor so that he issues you with a medical certificate, saying you have to do a battery of tests urgently. Afterwards, he can certify it was a false alarm. You may care to write that down. April, next year."

The man took out his wallet, and paid him, and left smiling.

* * *

The next person was a woman about fifty, smartly dressed, fine bones to her face, arresting eyes, but a lined, anxious mouth.

"My son is twenty-eight and is going to get married shortly, in Chile. His fiancé is South American. I haven't met her, but I am worried and upset, I can't explain why, I just feel uneasy about the whole thing."

"Give me a minute, will you?"

Aldous sat loosely, probing.

"Your future daughter-in-law is of Spanish descent, with three-eighths Indian and one-eighth-Chinese. Your son is attracted because she is the antithesis of Swedish values but you will find it impossible to adapt to her. You would find very much of what she says to be inaccurate. She will leave the breakfast dishes, and the lunch dishes, and wash up last thing at night."

The woman grimaced.

"In five and a half years he will leave her and her son and return to Sweden. If you interfere now, he will never forgive you, but when he comes back to Sweden, he will live with you for some years. He will marry again, with a Swedish woman, and you will have a good relationship with her."

"So I don't go to the wedding? I don't fly to Chile?"

"That is what you have come to ask me and the answer is don't."

She paid him, turned impulsively in the doorway and said, "Thanks," then gave him a stiff smile and went.

* * *

Half an hour later, the bell rang, and Aldous opened to a handsome, strong woman of about thirty-five, casually dressed in a jersey, who looked at him with frank assessment, and was shown to a chair.

Aldous said, "Your husband is a ship captain and you're worried about something happening to him?"

She held back her surprise and said, "I'm impressed."

Aldous said, "He is safe. He will never die at sea, but in his bed."

She joked, "He won't die with his sea boots on."

"Indeed, he won't."

He looked at her thoughtfully.

"You have three children, but you want to have another?"

She nodded.

Aldous jerked in his chair. She wanted to have a child by him, a child who would be psychic!

He said carefully, "You would like to have another child, but a child, who is psychic. However, having intercourse with a psychic doesn't automatically produce a psychic child. It happens only with specific acts of intercourse."

"And when would such an act of intercourse be successful?"

Her smile was mocking.

"Your husband will be away three more days. Then he will be here for five days. Intercourse taking place just after his departure would be successful."

She smiled.

"Give me your phone number, and I'll call you."

"Do you think some practice first is a good idea?"

"Indeed, but I leave tomorrow."

She pouted.

"The plane tickets are booked."

She wrote her name and phone number.

They stood up, he drew her to him, and kissed her hotly.

Drawing apart, he led her to the door.

Afterwards, he went into the living-room, and found Annika there.

She grinned. "Being the Boy Scout and doing good deeds, eh? It's nice you don't always change."

Her mother called her, and she hurried out of the room.

103

Perhaps Gulliver wouldn't come to Gothenburg airport. Perhaps he'd just go away.

That afternoon they flew a thousand kilometres up the north-east coast to Umeå. Laden with their packs, they took the bus to Amäs, where an old friend, Sven Lindberg, met them with his four-wheel drive. Years ago, Aldous had warned him that Sven's father had prostate cancer, and saved his father's life. They drove to the shops, where they stocked up on food, then drove down to their cottage beside the lake. Sven came in and sat down comfortably, while the family were busy. The ground floor had a kitchen against one wall, a long table in the middle, with chairs, and at the far end, a door led into a bedroom with a double bed.

A wooden stairway, with a rail, led upstairs, to one long room with eight beds around the walls.

Sven said, "Are you going to take the canoes – you must be out of training? Your shoulders are going to hurt!"

"Maj-Britt has this rowing machine in one of the rooms with all that diabolical gym apparatus. I've got another one in London, and another down in Spain. But these aren't exactly the same muscles. We'll only do a couple of hours the first day. None of these gym machines are any good for the exact movement of paddling a canoe," and they laughed.

Sven said, "I got up here a couple of weeks ago. We did a hike to near Savsjön and then up to Klysterberg and then up near Risliden. Slept out five nights, and took it easy. But that pack on my back! And I'd gone out for half-an-hour five nights running back home."

His wife came over, and they had the evening meal together.

They made it an early night.

104

They loaded their packs, tents and food into plastic, watertight barrels and lashed them into the sixteen-foot canoes, then put on the red life jackets which irritated Aldous. No self-respecting Swede would be seen in a canoe without one, and if a warden saw you without it, you could get a severe reprimand.

He and Maj-Britt moved with a slow stroke towards the far side of the kilometre-wide Amjö lake, the forested hills rising up on the far side. The girls moved swiftly ahead, wide ripples spreading in a fan behind them. As they drew further away, Aldous sent a sharp shout across the water, and their daughters cheekily turned their canoe around towards them and sat still waiting for them.

When they drew alongside, Maj-Britt said, "All right, all right! You're thirteen and fifteen and we're not! Have you finished showing off? You're going to be sore tonight!"

They crossed, then held in to the bank, came to the end of the arm of the lake and turned into the north-south lake.

A few white clouds drifted in a blue sky, not lazily but not to be hurried. The sun made them sweat, and then a light breeze cooled them. They worked up the eastern bank, looking at the pine trees, like rigid sentinels, unyielding dark green, guarding mysteries on the slopes beneath their rows. They would paddle around small headlands, the trees spaced out, the grass inviting, with scattered outcrops of granite, and splashes of colour. They would cut across open water, looking at the hills rise, now dark green, now dark blue, with the chasing sunlight and shadow from the clouds.

After an hour and a half, the lake narrowed to a stream, and Aldous called a halt.

They drew the canoes into birch woods, where the trees were few, the ground almost flat, carpeted with plants that came almost to their knees, a group of granite boulders rising to the height of a man.

They unloaded the waterproof barrels, unpacked, set up two domed tents, and Maj-Britt and the girls got lunch ready.

Aldous pulled out a groundsheet, threw it on the thick undergrowth and lay back on a springy cushion of vegetation with relief.

The years told! North of Thunder Bay, he had hardly paddled – not paddled two weeks.

After lunch, having lived for years in Spain, he had a siesta.

Maj-Britt sat with her back to a tree while the girls went exploring.

They came back, and while Maj-Britt and Annika stopped at the camp, Aldous and Lena went exploring, heading away from the water.

As they climbed through fir trees, the undergrowth thinned, and walking was easier. They came to groves of silver-trunked birches, the trees twisted, and often climbed over flat rock.

Near the top, they came to a well-marked track.

Aldous broke a branch to mark where they had joined it, and then they followed its slow turnings. Now they could breathe easily, and Lena said, "Which do you suppose you are most of, daddy, English or Canadian?"

"My father was English and we lived in Wiltshire. He died when I was twelve. My mother remarried – her husband was Canadian, so we went to live in Toronto. My first wife was Canadian, she died of incurable cancer when she was twenty-two. We were married only three years, and I was twenty-one when we got married. Her father had an important Portfolio Management Company in Spadina Ave near Sullivan St. One year after we got married, her parents were killed in a car crash, although I had warned them. Dorothy – that was her name, my wife – inherited the business and when she died of cancer, it became mine. Now, my three brothers had studied Business, so I gave the Toronto office to Claude."

"Uncle Claude," said Lena.

"The business grew awfully fast –"

"You were predicting the market," said Lena.

"I'm afraid so. Now I never do it, and when you grow up you must never do it either. Otherwise you could skew the whole thing. But, the thing is, we were able to open offices in Jersey and Torre Real, and my brothers George and Phil took them over."

"Uncle George and Uncle Phil," said Lena. "But they are managers – you own it all?"

"Something like that," agreed Aldous. "Now, you ask, am I English or Canadian? As you can see, that's an awfully complicated thing to answer. It's more than I can say. What would you think?"

"I suppose you're English on the ground floor, and Canadian upstairs. What do you suppose?" Lena wore a worried frown. "It must be hard to know where the one begins and the other ends. But do the Canadians believe you're Canadian, or do the English believe you're English?"

"Both things. So you see how complicated it is."

"It is," said Lena solemnly.

They had walked to high, rocky, open ground, with a view of distant hills and lakes, and stood and stared.

Aldous heard a voice behind them. "Tenemos compañia." The accent sounded Cuban.

He swung around and said, "Buenas tardes." Then he said in English, "Never expected to hear Spanish spoken here." He added, with a smile, "You aren't Cuban, are you, to make the whole thing even more incredible?"

"¡Compadre! ¡Como lo has adivinado!"

He laughed. "I wasn't really guessing. It was the accent."

"We've been living here for years, and speak Swedish, believe it or not. I thought perhaps our Spanish had a Swedish accent by now."

Aldous inclined his head gravely at the wife, then said, "What are Cubans doing in the middle of Västerbotton?"

"Castro, who else," said the wife, her face darkening.

The husband nodded. "We were lucky. We had a daughter working on the checkout at a Supermarket in Kansas. We went to visit her, as tourists, and she helped us get a suitcase with a thin false bottom. So, we went back. Then we put all our documents, the titles to our house and business in the false bottom. We shut up our house, switched everything off, pulled the curtains, locked the doors, and went through the airport check, on a second visit to our daughter, after six months since the first visit. I'm a pharmaceutical chemist, and I found a job with a Swedish company in the States. I kept begging for a transfer to Sweden, and now we're here with our daughter."

"In heaven's name, how did your daughter get out?"

"She went to the States to study, fell in love and married an American. All above board. They even came back to Cuba to put all the papers in order, following instructions from the Cuban Embassy. But although we've got all our titles to our property, we'll never see it again. You can't imagine what a last glimpse of your own house is like..."

The four stood in a silent communing, staring at the forests and lakes of northern Sweden, at the shadings and tints of colour.

Then Aldous shook hands warmly with them, and he and Lena headed back down the track, till they found the broken branch, and plunged into the forest.

* * *

Next morning, with sore shoulders, they paddled into a wide, smooth stream, with park-like trees, the banks covered the with grass and moss and wood anemones down to the glassy water. The trees muted the sunlight, and threw shade over the canoes.

They came out into a long, narrow lake, and staying by the edges, reached another stream, the Vormström. Halfway up, they stopped to make coffee and eat chocolate, then went on till they broke into another lake, the Vormträsket. On the west bank they could see Vormjuar, which soon slipped behind as they entered another stream, where the sunlight streaked down into a cathedral of tall trees. They saw a wide, flat stretch of grass, and pulled up the canoes and pitched their tents.

Maj-Britt was flattened, so the girls got up a late lunch, with meatballs and potatoes and vegetables.

All four had big appetites.

* * *

On the fifth day they reached Ruskjö Lake, where they stocked up on food, for the return.

Six days later, flying south, Aldous thought of the Cuban couple.

Life ambushed you.

Sometimes people saw it coming. Mostly they were blind.

But the suffering never stopped. And what was it all for?

Mankind's leaders laid ambushes that could be horrific. Their evil could increase exponentially...

In a cosmic machination, people were so pitilessly contrived that they seldom or never saw where they were heading.

He stared out of the plane window at clouds close to and level with the plane, and remembered the British Everest Expedition, in 1972 was it? Pete Boardman and Sherpa Pertemba had just left the summit of Everest, and met with Mike Burke coming up, much to their surprise. Mike was maybe ten minutes away from the summit. If he went on, he was going to die. If he turned back with Boardman and Pertemba, he'd live. They must have been about the same height as his plane window was now. Aldous shook his head, dazed. Mike *didn't* know. He went on for that ten minutes to the summit, and was never found. Aldous shook his head, trying to clear it. What sort of incubus was this life, with everyone wearing a blindfold, what affliction landed on man with a demonic derision by who? or by what?

Would Gulliver be there?

Two hours after reaching the house in Aschebergsgatan, Aldous rang the wife of the ship captain. She arrived half an hour later, and as she entered the flat, he caught her in his arms, covering her face with kisses. They stumbled to the bedroom, where he pulled her light sweater over her head, then slowly and agonisingly unbuttoned her blouse and. pulled it off her. He reached around and undid her bra; and lifted it from her arms and shoulders. He cupped her breasts, shudders running through him. Her breasts were full, and still resilient. He stroked her nipples, and then ran his hands down to undo her slacks. They dropped around her feet, and she stepped out of them adroitly, while he peeled down her panties. She stepped out of those as he pulled off his dressing-gown, and then he slid his hand between her legs, caressing her.

Her breath suddenly came sharply, and grew to panting. She fell on the bed, pulling him after her. He still stroked her and she cried in Swedish a phrase he had learnt well – "Put it in! Put it in!"

He slid into her honeyed lubricity and cupped her buttocks. Her excitement grew, feeding his own, and in his inflamed violence, her buttocks felt larger and larger. In short minutes, he came, and collapsed on her.

He lay there till his panting stopped, then gently caressed her belly. Soon it would round out, get heavy and taut, ripen...

He covered her lips with kisses, and penetrated her again.

Aldous met Gulliver at Gothenburg Airport.

Then Aldous rang Phil in Torre Real.

"Phil, how are you? Aldous here."

"Where are you?"

"At Gothenburg Airport."

"Aldous, they've been here from the British Embassy in Madrid, hoping to find you. Apparently, the police in London desperately need to talk to you."

"Phil, it's a business I don't want to get involved in. I prefer they manage without me. For heaven's sake, don't say you've talked to me. I'm flying down there today. Do you think someone could pick me up at Malaga Airport at seven pm?"

"No problem, but you know the Spanish Airways. If they delay the flight from Madrid to Malaga..."

"Let me think a moment..."

After a pause of a minute, Aldous said, "The plane will be on time."

"A miracle!"

"Phil, there's another thing."

"Go on."

"You know that our mother was married in England, to my father. When she became a widow, she went to Canada, remarried, and had you three."

"Aldous, please! Get to the point. What are you waffling about?"

"Phil, my father – in England – not your father, naturally – well, my father, before he married our mother – well, he had another son. My half-brother. I don't know whether he divorced that lady or whether it was a love-affair. Well, we met by accident in the wilds of the north of Canada, and – err – he's the spitting image of me. His name is Gulliver Windsor, and I need not say, my own surname is Windsor. It was a small frontier town sort of thing."

Phil's voice was strangled. "My God!"

"I'm bringing him with me. He's dying to meet you all. He's a geologist. Was a freelance, prospecting in the Australian outback."

"I'll meet you myself at Malaga Airport," Phil exploded. "Honestly, I

110

can hardly take this in. See you! I've got some people here with me. Bye!"

At Malaga Airport, they collected their luggage, and made their way out.

Aldous saw Phil, dressed in a dark, alpaca suit, impeccably tailored, with a tailored white cotton shirt, open at the neck. Phil was ten years younger, slim, tall, and with a spare, incisive face. He was as meticulous as his brother Claude, in Toronto; but with quick, Spanish-like gestures and alert eyes.

He came over, hugged Aldous, and shook Gulliver's hand, then stood back and looked at him, smiling.

"Two chips off the same block, it's amazing. Welcome to the family, Gulliver. Did you ever suspect of our existence?"

"I knew I had a brother, but my mother had lost all contact. When I asked her for his name, she said she didn't remember. I suppose I could have gone to the Registry in London and looked up the birth certificates but I've spent most of my life out of England." He smiled charmingly.

"Are you psychic like Aldous?"

"A little bit," Gulliver confessed.

"Did Richard give you the name Gulliver, or do you suppose it might have been your mother?"

Phil spoke with a very slight Spanish intonation, and he asked unselfconscious direct questions as the Spanish were wont to.

"Whoever it was, they must have been wishing travels upon me."

"Aldous tells me you've been all over, so they must have been on the right track."

"Do you like living in Spain?"

"I miss Canada, but I think I'd rather be here than anywhere else."

"And you have a Portfolio Management Office. Aldous tells me Torre Real is pretty small."

"And pretty rich. We get the filthy rich from Marbella and from Fuengirola. We're in the middle. Does your gift extend to psychic prediction of the markets? Aldous is hopeless."

"Well, I don't know," said Gulliver thoughtfully. "Let me think... a decade of growth in North America, and now a flattening for some time to come. That's what I see. The property markets in the north of Spain –" He laughed apologetically, and smiled disarmingly. "Not really my strong point, I'm afraid."

"That's remarkably good," said Phil. "Remarkable."

He led them out to the car.

Driving to Torre Real, he said, "The ladies are on tenterhooks, waiting to meet you. Big flap! Both Aldous and I have Spanish wives. My wife's name is Marivel, and we've got two small children, with dual nationality, of course. But I'm like Aldous, I've kept my Canadian nationality, although Aldous has two passports – a British one and a Canadian."

"I've got Australian and British. The Australians won't let you have any other passport beside their own, and I had to hand in my British one, but back in London, I simply applied for a new British passport and got it." Gulliver smiled pontifically.

It was hot. When Phil got in the car, he had taken off his coat, and hung it inside the back door. They drove with the windows down, to catch a breeze.

The car turned into Torre Real, and drove along the seafront promenade, *Paseo de la Costa*, then turned into the town and drove by luxurious hotels, apartment buildings and villas in landscaped gardens.

The streets rose, and on the outskirts of the town, with the countryside sloping up to nearby hills, they turned into Calle Alhaurin.

Aldous' house stood in a large garden, with trees, and Phil swung into the circular drive. A Hispano-Suiza was parked outside, and Gulliver leaned forward to look.

Phil said, "That's a Hispano-Suiza, built before the Spanish Civil War. It's a museum piece, worth its weight in gold. It's the size of a locomotive, guzzles petrol like a drunken sailor, and stops other car drivers and all tourists dead in their tracks. It belongs to Aldous' father-in-law. Luckily, he drives it only a few kilometres, or he'd he ruined paying for gas."

A wide veranda ran, along the front of the house, with steps.

Perspiring, they got out of the car, collected their luggage and climbed up.

The carved oaken door opened suddenly and Aldous' wife rushed out.

"Anna!" he cried, and took her in his arms.

"Aldous!" she sobbed. "You cruel, heartless man. I haven't seen you for two months." She pouted tragically, then with a dazzling smile turned to Gulliver, and gave him an incredulous glance of cool assessment. Her smile broke out again.

"I'd swear you were fraternal twins. Gulliver, this is marvellous. I welcome you into the family. Our home is your home. I've got to be dreaming. Another brother-in-law, and you look so like Aldous! To think of the years – all the years – we have lost, without knowing you. Are you

112

married? I can't wait to meet your wife."

Phil smiled indulgently, and said, "You're overwhelming the poor man. Gulliver, you can accept her words very seriously. Family is everything in Spain, and now this family *is* yours in a way that is only possible in Spain."

Gulliver put on a bewildered expression. "I can't believe I have such a beautiful sister-in-law. Aldous, can I give her a kiss, do you think?"

Anna presented her cheek, and he kissed her. She said coquettishly, "You're just saying that about my being beautiful to flatter me."

"I've never pecked the cheek of a more beautiful woman in my life," he assured her.

"You and I are going to get on famously, just famously," said Anna, leading them into the house.

Anna was thirty-six, black hair, black eyes, a sensual, vivacious mouth, dressed like a Parisian model, with the lean, sinuous body of an upper-class Spanish woman.

They entered the foyer, with its white marble floor, and pieces of modernist sculpture. Leaving their suitcases to the maids, they went into the living-room, crowded with people staring at them expectantly. It was a huge room, with wall-to-ceiling windows, the walls done in lime, lined with pictures mainly from the Barcelona *Sala Pares* School... Roca Sastre, Duran, Busom, Mundo and others.

Aldous' three children rushed forward and pushed him onto one of the sofas done in ivory tapestry. Mateo sat in his lap, Jorge formally beside him, and Carla flung her arms around his neck.

A man of seventy came up to Gulliver, said, "I'm Leonardo, Anna's father," and took his hand. "I welcome you into this family, and wish to tell you how sorry we are that we never found you earlier."

Gulliver said, "And I thank you. I am honoured. You would be the owner of the Hispano-Suiza I saw?"

"You noticed it," said Leonardo, very pleased. "It is Spain's answer to the Rolls Royce."

A lady in her fifties, dressed simply but expensively, wearing jewellery, joined them, looking expectantly at Leonardo.

"This is my wife, Milagros, Anna's mother."

Despite the lines in her face, she had clearly been a great beauty.

Gulliver bent his head over her hand and kissed it, and gave her a warm smile.

"Well," said Gulliver, "It has been worthwhile travelling so far to find such a family."

Milagros beamed.

Leonardo was tall, athletically built for his years, and had a patrician face with a Roman nose. His expression was vestigially roué.

"Milagros, everyone wants to meet him. Let us begin with Aldous children..."

Carla was 13, Jorge 12 and Mateo eight. They got formally to their feet, and shook hands. All three were psychic. Gulliver felt Jorge probing, so he led him off the earth, out into space, across light years and onto his own planet, and confronted him for an instant with inconceivable wisdom and knowledge of the Confederation. The boy's eyes widened. His mind recoiled in stupor and withdrew his probe. His face whitened.

Aldous got up, and joined Leonardo and Milagros in introducing him to the guests.

Phil's wife, Marivel, was slim, with an engaging, intelligent and inquisitive face. Juan Trias and his wife, Luisa, were in their seventies, and came from Catalonia.

Aldous sent to Gulliver, "His grandfather owned a bank in Barcelona, which they sold. They bought apartment buildings along the *Gran Via*, but sold them before the Civil War and. got the money out to France. Under Franco, they invested in business, and now they own property around here as well."

Juan Trias was a tall, heavily-built man, with a large, alert face, and like Leonardo, had a beak of a nose. He sized up Gulliver with a lazy smile, and shook hands warmly.

Their granddaughter, Teresa, was twenty-five, with finely sculpted, distinguished features. Aldous sent to Gulliver, "She's into human rights. Belongs to Amnesty."

Carolina was about forty-five, her face ravaged over a fine bone structure. She welcomed Gulliver to Spain, and introduced her daughter, Carmen.

Aldous sent to Gulliver, "Carolina had five daughters, but four became drug addicts. One committed suicide. Carmen never got into drugs – she's a history teacher. Carolina goes to the Casino every day, and when they can, Leonardo and my wife go with her."

Everyone settled on the sofas, and Aldous probed his wife.

She had a young Italian lover, about twenty-four, a jet-setter. He made love to her every morning, several times, till she grew sore, and had to use a vaginal ointment. No AIDS. The Italian had a flat in Marbella. He went to the beach at midday, and in the afternoon made love to a wealthy American girl, about twenty-one. In the afternoons, Anna went to the beach, or to the Casino with Carolina – when she wasn't shopping or visiting.

Each sofa held five people, placed before a large picture window of armoured glass – the house was protected because of the paintings and sculptures.

Gulliver looked at the countryside and the hills beyond, and asked, "Do they farm that land, or is it all given over to tourism and villas?"

Anna said, "They farm a bit, but most of the peasants left years ago, to

114

work in the factories in the north of Spain, or in northern Europe."

Teresa, the Amnesty activist, said, "The land question down here was an unmitigated tragedy, and had a lot to do with Franco's military rebellion. The peasants were clamouring for land and for more wages, and the *caciques* were frightened."

"*Caciques*?"

"Local bosses and exploiters," said Leonardo. "I was only eight when the Civil War began, but my father was a *cacique*, and what was worse, a *latifundista*. That is to say, he owned so much land, as far as the eye could see and further, it was called a *latifundia*. Thank God, the peasants all left. I sold the land for building."

Aldous sent to Gulliver, "And the money he's made!"

"Those peasants now are living in, say, Barcelona, or Germany, or France. In Barcelona, say, they're living in Hospitalet or San Marti or suburbs like that, with tree-lined streets. They own their flats and drive cars. Otherwise, I wouldn't be able to raise my head and look anybody in the eye."

Teresa said, "Spain's leaders – it's so horrible, you can't imagine."

Juan, her grandfather, said, "That goes for leaders anywhere, my dear, in every country."

Gulliver said, "You don't think leaders lead?" and everyone looked at him strangely.

"Oops!" thought Aldous. He sent to Gulliver, "Remember you're a human with forty-five years experience of life!"

"Where have you been?" asked Carmen, with a seductive smile. "In the Outback or somewhere?"

"In the Outback," confessed Gulliver, managing to look rueful. "I'm a geologist."

Teresa said, "But you must have heard about Rwanda – and now it's Kosovo. It never ends."

"What was the trouble with the land and the peasants around here?" asked Gulliver, leaning forward intently.

Carmen said, with a shiver, "There were between two and three million landless day-labourers, who lived *abjectly*. In the cities, there were the same number of industrial workers, whose lives were equally abject. The factory owners were terrified of them asking for more wages. Down here on the land, there were another two million miserable peasants who share-cropped, or if they were lucky, owned smallholdings. Then Spain had about another two million who were middle-class or petite bourgeoisie – and lording it over everyone down here, there were fifty thousand *latifundia*, big landowners. In Seville, five percent of the landowners controlled seventy percent of wealth coming from the land. With the agitation among the dispossessed, things were ripe for the military revolt to protect the wealthy, the Church, the whole establishment. But I must be boring you. I'm a history teacher, so my tongue

115

runs away with me."

Gulliver implored her, "Please go on; I'm fascinated. Fascinated and appalled."

Everyone wanted to talk at once.

Juan Trias got in first. "The land problem in this country was one of centuries, and the core of Spain's politics. In other countries, the middle classes and the petite bourgeoisie revolutionised politics and took over. Here they failed, because they couldn't redistribute the land, so Spain festered. While the rest of the West forged ahead, we became a European backwater."

Luisa Trias said, shaking her grey head at the memory, "I know a shoemaker here. His grandfather was a small-holder, and one day the *cacique's* thugs carried him into the village more dead than alive, on the back of a mule. They'd beaten him up, and tied his hands behind his back, and they paraded the mule through the village to put the fear of God into the villagers. The Town Hall was run by the *cacique*, who said the grandfather hadn't paid his taxes. So the thugs, with shotguns, tried to seize his ploughing cows, and he put up a fight. He couldn't live without them."

Leonardo's wife, Milagros, told Gulliver, "We're saying villages, but the most any village consisted of was hovels and huts unfit for animals."

Carmen, the history teacher, was exerting all her charms on Gulliver. She said, "There were two great emigrations – one in 1911 and the next in 1920. They went to South America, poor people, and heaven only knows how they are living today. Some did make money and came back – we call those ones the *Indianos*. There was nothing here for them. When Luisa told you about the hovels in the villages, you have to think that a lot were living in huts out in the countryside."

Teresa, the activist, said, "General Primo de Rivera brought in a dictatorship between 1923 and 1927, and that made things much worse. The *caciques* were even more powerful than before. You couldn't talk freely and criticise. The peasants had to shut up. They had begun forming Unions and socialist parties, and they were shut down."

Leonardo said, "The nightmare was the Guardia Civil. They were ruthless, they inspired terror. When there were strikes, they'd ride into a village and hunt down the villagers, galloping after them into the countryside." He added, "Teresa, I think the Primo dictatorship might have lasted till 1930, I'm not sure."

Teresa laughed. "I'm not sure either."

They both turned to Carmen, who squirmed. Carmen said, "I'm not sure. I'd really have to look it up."

Carolina smiled at her daughter with approval, and said to Gulliver, "You're really interested in all this?"

Gulliver assured her, "You can't imagine how much. What happened after Primo?"

Carolina said, "Spain got a mild dictatorship under Berenguer. Political parties were allowed again, and hope awoke among the peasants around here. There was a Union close to here that had about 500 members in a few days after the Berenguer government legalised it. It grew to almost 2,000 in July, 1936, when Franco struck, and there were only some 7,500 peasants... The day laborers came running to join. The landowners paid them only a couple of coins for a day's work, so they lived lives of slow starvation. They remembered that the Union had got them more money, but Primo stopped that, and the landowners ground them underfoot again."

Anna said, "And to think of the dinner we'll have tonight." She turned to Gulliver. "We don't dine till nine-thirty. Are you hungry? Would you prefer we begin earlier?"

"We ate on the plane from Oslo to Madrid," he told her, "but thanks for the thought."

Aldous said, "A hovel stood where this house is now. They were day labourers, who didn't live in the village. I've seen them – thin as sticks and wrinkled beyond belief."

Teresa Trias asked him, "By 'seen', do you mean psychic 'seeing'?"
Aldous nodded.

Teresa said firmly, "I can't believe that. I just can't. It makes no sense. No one can deny the evidence of our senses or the reality of the world around us. Next thing, you'll be bringing aliens into the house!"

There was a general laugh.

Aldous said, "You've got a worn piece in the gears of your Vespa, or whatever you call it. At the end of this week, you'll have to send it to the garage for repairs."

Teresa looked shocked.

"*Touché*," smiled her grandfather.

Luisa said, "You see, your grandfather 'believes'. Now he'll make you a bet. If he's wrong, he'll pay. If Aldous is right, you'll pay."

Juan smiled genially, and Teresa shook her head.

Anna said, "In 1931, the Republicans won, and on April 12, the King left Spain. Meanwhile, the *caciques* had declared they'd won, but when the republic was declared, they were finished. They forbad demonstrations in the village streets, so all the landless villagers crowded into the bars to celebrate.

"Everything changed. You could get married outside of the church. The church was no longer allowed to go into business, and could not teach. A day-labourer got 3.50 pesetas a day, but now it was raised to 5 pesetas a day, and just before the Civil War in 1936, to 7 pesetas a day. The trouble was that day-labourers couldn't get work every day, but still, they could buy fish and flour, rice and sugar and olive oil."

Gulliver said, "So it was the Third World, but they escaped, while the rest of Third World just sinks down further."

117

"That's right!" cried Teresa.. "I've got all sorts of folders and articles I can show you."

"Will I see you tomorrow?" asked Gulliver eagerly.

Aldous said, "I was thinking of going to the beach tomorrow morning – Anna, Gulliver, myself. Do you want to join us Teresa? Marivel?"

Phil said, "I've got to work. Will you be calling in the office, Aldous?"

"Tomorrow afternoon."

Jorge cried, "And what about me and Carla and Mateo?"

"Don't you want to come?" said Aldous with feigned disappointment.

"Of course we do!" cried Carla.

"So what was Franco trying to save?" asked Gulliver.

"Franco lusted for power," said Milagros, Aldous' mother-in-law. "He saw he could have the support of the landowners, the factory owners – all those disgusting people scared witless at paying a couple of pesetas more per hour. He saw his chance for absolute power, and after he won, he shot about a quarter of a million people, just to show how powerful he was. He used to walk around under a pallium – a canopy, held up on four poles by four men – a privilege reserved for high Princes of the Church. This dwarf of a man, about five-foot high, with a pot belly and little cherries between his legs, a million deaths behind him, strutting under the gold cloth of a pallium!"

Leonardo exploded, "Milagros! For God s sake! What language!"

"If you survive to my age, you can say what you like," she declaimed to the company.

"Bravo!" cried Luisa Trias. "Speaking as someone of the same *quinta* – the same age group – I couldn't agree more."

Gulliver said carefully, "I've never given thought to this of politicians and leaders. Well, you know, I've been isolated. But you Spanish seem to have a thing about leaders –"

"It's everybody everywhere!" said Teresa Trias heatedly. "That's why I belong to Amnesty International. Leaders in Spain are – and have been – awful, but they are no better outside. Take that Clinton. In Rwanda, they murdered 800,000 people. With about 5,000 Western troops, it could have been avoided. The Secretary General of the United Nations was Boutros Boutros-Ghali, and in his Memoirs, he tells us that in May 1994, he went to the White House to plead with Clinton for action. Clinton brushed aside what he was saying, and started on Clinton's picked candidate for – the Director of UNICEF! While 800,000 died, hacked to death, Clinton worried about getting his own man into the United Nations Children's Fund!"

Gulliver paled.

"The whole international set-up for human rights is a ramshackle business, thanks mainly to Clinton. Eighty-five countries have offered troops for a Rapid Reaction force when a genocide is going to happen. Clinton has stymied it. Right now, 85,000 troops could mobilise." Teresa was flushed, and very angry.

The dining-room held a big circular table of dark, highly polished wood.

It was set with table mats, silverware, crystal.

Anna turned out the lights, and lit candles.

They had *gazpacho*, followed by cold, baked salmon with cold vegetable pie, followed by silver salvers with small Andalusian sweet cakes, in a score of varieties.

They drank *Bach Extrissimo*, and had *Jerez* with the cakes.

* * *

They went to bed at one o'clock. In his bedroom on the second floor, Gulliver sat in a chair, made himself comfortable, and sent out a probe, looking for Clinton.

He entered his mind, and probed systematically for fifteen minutes.

Then he searched for Tony Blair, who was sleeping, and probed. He switched to Yeltsin; then the other European leaders, one after the other. Then he sought out the leaders of China, Japan, India and Pakistan.

It was three o'clock in the morning.

He pressed his wristwatch, and transmitted:

Urgent. Gulliver reporting:

Have probed the minds of the world leaders. THEY ARE IN IT FOR THEMSELVES.

Secondarily, they defend the interests of their own countries over that of other countries.

They directly contravene our Codex, given from the First Dimension, that a leader shall lead the led to Higher Ground.

They are utterly incapacitated for this task.

The most powerful leader is Bill Clinton, amoral and immoral. While 800,000 Rwandans were being butchered, the United Nations Secretary

General came to him for help. Some 5,000 Western troops were needed. Clinton waffled on about his nominee for a Children's Fund!

Under Clinton, the inequality between the rich nations and the Third World has grown to unconscionable disparities.

The Third World suffers starvation, disease and ignorance.

Humankind is clueless and adrift. Leaders sweep humans into vaster agglomerations which are rudderless in unison. Leaders' aimless stupidity – except when they are murderous – pushes this planet astray into a drift.

Next morning, Aldous and Gulliver had breakfast on the back lawn, beside the swimming pool.

Aldous said, "Leonardo and Milagros are not married. Leonardo was married to the daughter of a grandee of Spain, and they had two children. They separated, but divorce was impossible – the Roman Catholic Church had Spain in an iron grip. Milagros had been an actress and was incredibly beautiful. Leonardo had been ostracised, but he didn't care. He had all these women from the working-class. He set up house with Milagros and they had Anna. Now, in those days, if you weren't married, you were not allowed to put the father's surname on the birth certificate. The child had to have the mother s surname, proclaiming to the world that the child was illegitimate. Of course, Franco kept this; he put the country back forty years. But up in Catalonia, above all in Barcelona, the Registrars turned a blind eye. They simply registered what you wrote down. You gave the place and date of your 'wedding' and they didn't ask for a Marriage Certificate. Milagros had Anna in a Barcelona hospital. The midwife nurse was nosey as hell, and Leonardo told her to get lost. He wrote down the name and date of birth of the baby, the names of the parents and made her sign. He said he'd fill out the rest later. She was a rude Catalan – they are very rude up there, apparently – but he treated her with aristocratic indifference.

"So, Anna and I are not married either. Anna adores her parents, and if they couldn't get married, she was damned if she would throw a marriage in their faces. She made it very clear they were all in the same boat.

"Anna and I disappeared for six weeks, saying we were going to London. When we came hack, we said we'd had a private wedding at a Registry Office in London."

Anna came into the garden with Teresa, who carried a briefcase. They sat down, and the maid served them with croissants and coffee.

Teresa opened her briefcase to show Gulliver a pile of folders and documents. "Iniquity, all of it," she said. "The Third World, and the rich countries."

Gulliver scanned the papers eagerly. "I'll read this all this afternoon. I'll take this up to my room."

"You can keep the briefcase, if you give it back to me," Teresa said.

They went down to the beach with the children, and set up beach umbrellas. Anna waved to an elderly lady, who picked up her towel and bag and came over to join them.

Aldous sent to Gulliver, "She came of a good family, but never married. When the mother died, she had to go and live with her married brother, but the wife made life impossible. So she went into service with a *Marquesa*, in a palace, as nursemaid to the children. Nightmare life. She learned typing, found work in an office, and got into Social Security, so that now she has a pension – a pretty miserable sum. The Spanish Prime Minister isn't generous with his pensions. It's a Conservative government of rich parliamentarians who turn up their noses at the impoverished. She completely lost contact with all the friends of her girlhood and adolescence. She was *working*! Very infra dig. And a nursemaid! Then a typist! But by far the worst of it was not what she was doing, but that she was *working*. They had attitudes here that went back to when the riches came from the Indies in the great galleon fleets."

Gulliver scowled.

The lady was thin, with a deeply lined, sad face, and her movements were listless.

She sat down beside Teresa, who said, "Matilda, you're looking well."

"I love the summer. I see we're speaking English today." She peered. "Mr Windsor. I didn't see you. So you're back with us again. I hope you don't find it too hot."

Gulliver said, "You speak English very well."

"I was at a private Girls' College in England from the age of thirteen to sixteen." She smiled at him.

Teresa asked, "No problems?"

"Oh, dear. Eight years ago, I had the cistern fixed, and now it's dripping again. The country's so short of water, and they make such a fuss about saving water."

Teresa smiled at her. "Don't you worry. I'll call the plumber today."

"You'd think they could put in materials that *lasted*," Matilda lamented.

Gulliver remarked, "When agriculture was so important here, drought must have been a real problem."

Matilda said, "People starved."

Gulliver said, "But if all the agricultural workers have gone north, where does the food come from?"

Carla said, "We're in the European Union now, so it's all specialisation. It rains in northern Europe, so *they* do the agriculture and send us the food. The sun shines down here, so *we* give them suntans when they come on holiday."

Everyone laughed, and Teresa told Gulliver, "Spain still has its agriculture, but it's technological now."

A slim lady, with a vague expression on her face, came onto the beach, saw them, and walked over.

"Hello, Nieves. We're talking in English today."

"Oh, good, I'll practise."

She set out her towel, and sat down.

Aldous sent to Gulliver, "She was wealthy, with a marvellous house. She signed it over to her son, who's twenty-eight. He's a painter, who doesn't sell, and doesn't know Tuesday from Thursday. Her husband, Luis, gave the son papers to sign, which he signed without even looking at them. The he skipped out for South America, emptying the hank accounts, with the money from the house. Now she lives in a tiny flat."

Nieves looked at Gulliver. "What an amazing resemblance you have to Aldous."

"I'm his half-brother."

"Ah", she said, looking disoriented, then stretched out on the towel.

Aldous sent, "Luis, her husband, had the most enormous debts, so he fled."

Gulliver sent to Aldous, "Probe her mind and get a surprise."

Aldous did. All the legal papers declared the whereabouts of husband unknown, and that her own resources were nil. They had been stolen. But, in fact, Luis was up in Valencia, and when the hue and cry died down, Nieves would join him.

Aldous sent to Gulliver, "My God! And she's the very picture of inanity and 'I don't understand anything, poor me!' The son signed over the house, post-dating the documents, to rescue it from the creditors."

Aldous sat in the sun, admiring the firmness of Anne's topless breasts. He had made her sore again, last night.

He got to his feet. "I'm going for a walk along the beach."

"To look at all the topless women," jeered Carla.

"Young lady, more respect for your ageing parent."

"I'll come with you," said Jorge, and they walked slowly along the sand.

"There are some big ones," said Jorge.

"Big what, son?" asked Aldous.

"Big tits."

"Ah! So young and so observant. You promise well. I hope you're as observant at school."

"Dad, Gulliver's not your brother. He's just pretending."

"Amazing," said Aldous absently.

"With ordinary people, you can look at their minds like a large field. Gulliver's mind stretches right around the world and out into space."

"Lucky Gulliver," said Aldous. He added severely, "Psychic vision is a gift but you must never confuse it with a feverish imagination."

The boy walked sulkily beside his father.

He said, "Dad, I'm almost grown-up now. I'm twelve. What's going on?"

Aldous said soothingly, "Sometimes a psychic gift can go a bit off the rails and tell you funny things. It's not something you can control. In a way, it controls you. These mix-ups happen in adolescence, and then they go away."

Aldous stared a moment at three topless women, then swung sharply about, and led Jorge back to their beach umbrellas.

* * *

Teresa said, "I've never told you the story of how our family fortune was founded. It was up in Barcelona. My great-great grandfather lived in a little village, and he went to Barcelona looking for work. He found a job with a married couple who had a jewellers, in *Puerto del Angel*. He served the customers during the day, and at night, slept under the counter. As the years passed, the old couple treated him like an adopted son, and when they got old, they gave him the shop, in return for a weekly pension for them to live on. When they died, he sold the shop, and with the money traded on the Barcelona Stock Exchange, down in the *Lonja*, close to the Post Office.

"He was making money, so he put five employees, who were very loyal and who he trusted implicitly, in Madrid. One stayed on the *parquet*, on the floor of the Madrid Stock Exchange. Another ran up to the roof with trading results, and a third signalled with flags to a fourth who was on the roof of Our Señora of The Post, the Madrid Post Office. A fifth ran downstairs to send telegrams to Barcelona. Employees collected them, and ran across to the *Lonja*. So, Tomás, my great-great grandfather, knew what was happening with the Madrid shares in Madrid. As they were traded in Barcelona too, he bought and sold according the telegrams he was getting.

"Well, he made a fortune, and set up an important bank.

"And he fell in love."

Everyone was listening, and shaking their heads in surprise.

"Yes, he fell in love, but with the daughter of a Catalan aristocrat, a Catalan *Marques*, and Tomás knew the father was such a bigoted snob, he would never entertain his suit, although he *did* have a Bank. The father was a member of the exclusive and expensive *Circulo Equestre*, so Tomás joined too. He paid the doormen generously and when the *Marques* arrived, they would take his hat, his coat and his stick obsequiously, to put them away. Then they retrieved a written message from his daughter, Isabela, inside his hat band, and gave it to Tomás. Tomás would write an adoring note, which the

124

doormen inserted into the hat band, for the *Marques* to carry back home, where his loving daughter would greet him, and relieve him of his hat, his coat and his stick.

"Up in the Montseny mountains near Barcelona, Tomás bought a small, abandoned *Masia*, a Catalan farmhouse, and put workmen into it to rebuild the place. Sundays, he attended the tiny parish church in the small, remote village, and made generous donations to the priest. At Mass, he met the farmers and their families, and visited their lonely farms on the green, cloud enshrouded mountain tops. He told them that if they were sick, he would pay their costs, and he left money with the doctor in a nearby village.

"Now, the Spanish Catholic Church in its wisdom ordained that to get married, you had to publish Banns for three weeks, and you could marry only in your local church, or, paying a large donation, in one of the great fashionable churches. That made a secret wedding for Tomás and Isabela impossible.

"However! Tomás was now a resident on the top of a lonely Catalan mountain, and was respected by the rural priest.

"The priest agreed to marry him, a local resident, and the Banns were published – with the name of the daughter of the Marques there for all to see. Except that her name meant nothing to the hardy mountain farmers, used to keeping to themselves.

"Tomás bought a Hispano-Suiza – a car which never broke down, and early one Saturday morning, when Isabela went out, he drove her to the Masia, where her wedding dress had been waiting for some weeks. They went to the church, with many farmers' wives as witnesses, and the priest married them.

"Tomás had prepared a wedding reception in Barcelona, without telling his friends who it was he had chosen as his blushing bride. Saturday afternoon, his friends delivered invitations to the homes of Isabela's friends, together with a formal invitation and a loving note from Isabela to her father.

"Now, it would be apparent to everyone what had happened, but if the father attended, appearances would be saved, and no one could say a word.

"The *Marques*, with all the family, appeared, and with everyone's eyes upon them, warmly greeted Tomás and accepted him into the bosom of the family. Apparently, the *Marques* played his role splendidly... remembering he was a stiff-necked Spanish aristocrat."

"And you're the result," said Aldous admiringly. "It was well worth the struggle."

* * *

After lunch, Aldous told Gulliver that he wanted to go to his Brokers' Office, and Gulliver said he wanted to study the papers Teresa had brought.

* * *

Aldous walked into the Windsor Portfolio Management Company, and the employees nodded at him. He went to Phil's office, knocked and put his head in the door.

"Aldous! Come in." Phil spoke quickly to the lady standing in front of his desk. She gathered up papers, nodded to Aldous, and left.

"So we're doing well," said Aldous.

"And we're going to do better. This conservative government has given us a new law, with a new investment modality – Unit-Linked Life Insurance with Financial Portfolio. The big headache in investing in Spain is that when you sell, you have to pay twenty-percent tax, and that hurts. Now, for the clients of our company, you pay a monthly fee covering death insurance. The insurance itself need represent only a very few percent of the total portfolio investment the client makes. So, when you are under this fiscal umbrella, you can buy and sell on the Stock Exchange tax free. Without it, as I say, it costs you 20% of your gain on each sale.

"We also have another product, almost tax free, International SICAV. It's French and means 'Company' 'Investment' 'Variable', and it's bringing the good people of Marbella and its hinterland to our doors.

"The Company invests in the Stock Market and pays only 1% on gains. All participants in the Trust can sit on the Board, which can lead to a Tower of Babel if all decide to, but we have clients who just love that, but they know what they're talking about, so we have a friendly gathering of kindred spirits and improve our company image and our client relationships."

"Perfect," breathed Aldous. "God bless PP, or whatever the party calls itself. Long may they govern Spain."

Phil said dryly, "They'll he pleased to hear the expression of such sentiments. There are those who have something else to say."

He pulled out a folder of papers. "You may care to go over these. Incidentally, we finally got shot of those five people."

Five employees could not adapt to the new technologies.

Phil said, "We finally negotiated for a total of nine million pesetas severance compensation."

Aldous raised his eyebrows.

"It's the law in this country. It's about the one country in the world where you can't fire someone without it costing you a leg and an arm. Spanish judges are highly individualistic. They rule as they feel like. What the law says is another matter!"

"Come on," protested Aldous.

126

"Well, we've got five new people from Cataluña."

"Aren't they very rude, those people up there?"

"No idea. These five are polite, accurate, hardworking and they seem to feel deeply about money! In this part of Spain, the feeling seems to be that money is to be spent and enjoyed."

"Imagine," murmured Aldous.

"These Catalans seem to feel that money should be taken out of circulation and invested."

"A-ah!"

"So, over the next two years, there are six more people I want to ease out, and we'll bring more people from the north. Of course, even to think of firing someone is practically a crime in this country."

* * *

Aldous had a small office and he took the papers there to study them.

An hour later, the phone rang. It was Anna. "The police have rung. They want to talk to you. Can I give them this number?"

"Give it to them."

He hung up, and waited, then went and spoke to the receptionist. - -

* * *

They showed the two policemen into a clients' reception room, with a long, polished table and twelve chairs.

One of the *Policia Nacional* was a Sergeant, and he said, "We have a case of a missing girl, aged 21. She disappeared three weeks ago, leaving her home at 10 pm and saying she would be back at midnight. She is from Marbella. You will understand the reactions of the parents, and the Press has taken it up. The parents make constant statements to the Press, and we have made no progress, as you may imagine."

He laid a big briefcase on the table."

"Could you help us?" and he smiled briefly, "as you have in the past. Here is some of her clothing, if it would help you get a feeling about her."

Aldous shook his head.

"Give me a photo."

They handed him a large colour photo, and he stared at it four minutes.

He said finally, "I see a car driving from Pedro de Alcántara, driving away from the sea – driving towards Ronda – there are two young men – they aren't part of her usual circle of friends – she calls them Pedro and José. They turn off on a dirt road, to the right of the road, and go about a kilometre. They force her out of the car. One holds her arms while the other tries to rape her. He grabs her head – he bangs it on the ground – there is a rock in the ground – he fractures her skull. They look around – they find a natural rock trench – a short, narrow gap. They push her in there – they cover her with stones. I see very high ground, very high country. I see hunters – on the weekends."

The two *Policía Nacional* nodded sombrely. "How far up the road?"

"Some distance, some distance –"

They thanked him, and took their leave.

Aldous was sweating freely, his shirt wet.

When Phil hurried in, he cried, "My God, are you okay? What's happened?"

"A murder. I think I've pinpointed it. I think so..."

He got up tiredly. "Phil, I'll give you back those papers. I'm going back home. I need a shower."

Phil exclaimed, "Was it that girl from Marbella, the one the papers are full of?"

"I think so."

"Hell! You've solved it!"

"I dunno. They haven't found her yet. Now they'll have to take dogs in, and we'll see."

He gave the papers back, and when he walked out the employees were looking at him agog, wondering whether he was in trouble with the police.

* * *

At home, he had a shower, changed, drank three glasses of fruit juice, and went upstairs, to knock on Gulliver's door.

Gulliver let him in, and sent, "An ugly business. How you humans kill each other."

He waved to the folders Teresa had brought, and sent, "And this is an even uglier business. Are you recovered enough to drive me up into the hills? I have to transmit, but this human body of mine is clamouring to get out of the house, away from the air-conditioning, and into the country."

128

They left the car, and walked up a hillside with olive trees. The countryside was dotted with villas and shade trees, and the sea glittered distantly. They reached a stone wall, banking a terrace of earth, under the shade of an olive tree, and sat on the rough, grey stones.

Gulliver breathed deeply, in satisfaction, and said, "Isn't it hot! But the air here is clear - even though indecently humid!"

He pressed his watch, and said:

Urgent. Gulliver reporting:

The human brain is deeply flawed. I suspect that evolution on this planet has gone badly wrong, is flawed to begin with, and the human brain is its marred product.

The Third World suffers high death-rates, malnutrition, starvation, illiteracy and crime. It lacks money, credit and capital.

The fortunes of the world's 475 billionaires outstrips the income of the poorest HALF of all humans.

The latest UNITED NATIONS HUMAN DEVELOPMENT REPORT states that the combined wealth of the earth's richest billionaires, Bill Gates, the Sultan of Brunei and the Walton family of Wal-Mart exceed the combined GNP of the 43 least developed nations on the planet.

Your Excellencies, the United Nations report that in the last 50 years global GNP has soared from $3 trillion to $30 trillion, but the differences between rich and poor have got worse. The report asserts that 1.3 billion humans in the Third World live on less than one dollar a day.

In these years, some ten countries of the Third World have made certain advances. In the last 30 years, the rest have gone downhill.

These counties hold some 3 billion humans, struggling to survive in abject poverty.

Your Excellencies, since 1959, the rich countries have paid $1 trillion to poor countries, which has not helped them, but most of the money was not to raise them up. It was for strategic use. The USA has spent a greater part of that money on Israel – a well-to-do, militaristic country – Egypt and Columbia. The money has been used often for arms and for combating drug production.

Not all countries showed this flawed brain activity. Sweden spends a higher part of its GNP on aid than any other advanced country.

Aid from rich countries for the starving rose from about $20 billion in 1970 to a high point of $70 billion in 1991. Then aid fell to a trickle. Your Excellencies will find this incomprehensible, but I guarantee the facts. The blame lies with USA, the richest country on earth. The USA produces 30 percent of world output, but it gives only 17 percent of help. The advanced industrial democracies now hand out a figure below 0.25 percent of their GNP to help the starving majority of humans.

But within the wealthy countries themselves, this savagery persists. About 15 percent of Americans and about 17 percent of Europeans live below the designated poverty levels, and their wealthy neighbours in their physical neighbourhood do not lift a finger to help them. Your Excellencies, this maiming of the human brain is grave. I do not know what it is, because I have not yet studied the brain itself.

Welfare programs by governments to help the needy are mainly detested by local communities. People in comfortable circumstances think help only makes the needy more dependent; but here, as throughout the Galaxy, the Common Distribution Curve rules, and the bottom 15 percent of any human population is mentally handicapped or impaired in personality by the inevitable statistical distribution.

The Third World is punished in other ways.

Your Excellencies, twenty years ago, Third World countries like Indonesia, Philippines or Brazil and Chile had luxuriant tropical forests, valuable mineral resources, teeming seas of fish and fertile, agricultural land. Costa Rica has cut its forests for cattle runs, to export meat; Indonesia has cut them to foster palm oil production.

I have read a British government report which says, global warming, land degradation, deforestation, loss of biodiversity, polluted and over-fished oceans, shortage of fresh waters, population pressures and insufficient land on which to grow food will otherwise endanger the lives of everyone – rich and poor.

Until now, the rich countries have been successful in procuring clean water and air for themselves.

People living in rich countries rationalise their not helping by saying that it's money poured down the drain, when all the evidence shows that aid works.

However, the impaired human brain is controlled by the Selfish Gene Instinct. The rich want to reproduce their genes, and kill those of outsiders. Also, most curiously, something in the human brain makes people behave like a flock of sheep or a herd of cows. They try all to think alike. As with sheep and cows, the dominant animal leads, and the rest slavishly follow.

Among the world leaders, we have the same hierarchy. The leader of the most powerful country, Clinton, dominates the rest.

Your Excellencies, polls by USAID show that most Americans "believe that there is lots of waste and inefficiency" in aid programs "that could he slashed without cutting services."

This is so shockingly irrational that I can ascribe this only to defective human brains.

In Britain, the Department for International Development polled British leaders and discovered that most were afraid "that money rarely reached those who were in need."

Your Excellencies, the money rarely reaches those most in need because the money is not there in the first place.

The World Bank recently issued a report, ASSESSING AID, which, states bluntly that aid *can* be targeted and *can* tackle Third World poverty. It declares outright that the impact of aid "is large... One percent of GDP in assistance translates into a one percent decline in poverty and similar decline in infant mortality."

Margaret Thatcher, Helmut Kohl and Ronald Reagan propounded Free Trade at the beginning of the 1980s, and Clinton took up the banner. Free trade has been Free Plunder.

Free Trade imposed on the Third. World has hurt factory workers, small farmers and small businesses in the rich countries. Public opinion polls in USA showed the majority of Americans were unbelievers, and in 1998, a WALL STREET JOURNAL/NBC NEWS survey found that 58 percent of Americans polled thought that "foreign trade has been bad for the U.S. economy."

But Clinton has steamrollered on.

Free Trade instead of Aid has put the Third World deeply into debt. In 1996, the wealthy advanced countries created the Heavily Indebted Poor Countries Initiative, and named twenty-six countries for possible debt relief. Only a few countries received sparse relief.

In Cologne, the G-8 countries named 33 countries for relief, but only for a total of $15 billion. The rich countries, led by Clinton, want their pound of flesh.

The debt of the Heavily Indebted Poor Countries amounts to $127 billion. At Cologne, another proposal would have cut back that debt by $60 billion, but the US Congress blocked it.

On the one hand, the Selfish Gene Instinct makes the Third World procreate like rabbits, when there are no resources to feed these mouths. On the other hand, some sort of predator instinct in the rich countries makes them grind down the poor.

The unknown UFO Planet has placed a robot quarantine fleet around the earth to stop humans pushing out into space. Can Your Excellencies imagine how humans would treat planets less developed than themselves! Can

Your Excellencies imagine humans receiving the 15th level of Science and technology – what they would do to the Confederation!

I believe this is a matter for the Nine Planet Cabinet itself.

END

Aldous thankfully got to his feet. The stones had cut into his backside.

Gulliver said, "Let's walk."

"What is the Nine Planet Cabinet?"

"That seldom meets. It's more important than the Council. It is for emergencies."

"And what are these less developed planets?"

"Our nine planets found each other because they advanced to the point of sending signals into space – primitive, electronic signals, to be sure, something like Red Indian smoke signals. There are other planets at lower levels, but we can't find them. *However* –" he paused, looking around him. "*However*, sometimes you do stumble upon an inhabited planet with beings of emerging rationality – who certainly are going to evolve in time into rational, conscious beings."

"You seem to get around, you people," acknowledged Aldous.

* * *

Anna had rented the four videos of Star Wars, and before and after dinner, they watched the first two.

About midnight, Aldous and Gulliver sauntered out into the garden. When they were a distance from the house, Gulliver pressed his watch, and transmitted:

Urgent. Gulliver reporting:

Have seen films, *Star Wars*. These films show humans with advanced, faster-than-light starships, out in space. Murder and mayhem! Aliens are shown as grotesque figures – grotesque in human eyes – but some are close to true alien forms.

However, most 'aliens' are evil, malignant. The files project every human defect into the aliens themselves, and life in space is depicted as one of war, blazing weapons, evil surmounting evil.

I fear the films presage what would happen if humans get out of the solar system.

The humans show themselves as virtuous, killing and destroying to

protect their own untainted interests.
        END

"They're just films," protested Aldous.

"Indeed, they are. Just films," agreed Gulliver.

* * *

Next morning, down on the beach, Aldous asked Mateo, "How is school?"

"It's all right," said Mateo. "As I know who likes me, and who doesn't, or who is going to have a go at me, or who wants to bully me, I can keep out of the way. The trouble is, when the teacher asks a question, I can often read the answer in his mind, so I have to be careful."

"It makes you sick," declared Jorge. "I keep reading the teacher's mind. I want to work something out for myself, and the answer is there. I'm afraid I won't learn enough."

"So what happens in the exams?"

"I know enough to get by, and I know who the class stars are, so I can check their exam papers, what they're writing, or what they've written."

"And what about you, Carla?"

"I know what the boys are thinking about me. It's awful. So many are falling in love or undressing me –"

"So many!"

"Well, I can feel they're sort of on the edge –"

"And they undress you in their minds?"

"There's nothing I can do!"

"Then where are they all! You're down here on the beach, topless, in some string panties – where's the crowd?" He mimed putting his hand up to shade his eyes, and looking around the beach.

Carla pouted.

"I go to school in Marbella. They don't know I'm on this beach, that's all."

Aldous said, "Well, when you're so beautiful as that, I suppose you have to hide away."

"That's right," she said eagerly. "Oh, daddy, you *understand*."

"It's a cross you're going to have to bear," Aldous told her.

Anna looked narrowly at her daughter.

In Marbella, Aldous had a two-bedroom flat for Readings. The passageway opened on one side to a living-room, where he received the clients, and on the other to two bedrooms. One bedroom was furnished as a reception room.

That afternoon, Aldous and Gulliver went there, and Gulliver made himself comfortable in the reception room.

Aldous' first visitor was a young American woman, about twenty-three, with a faintly elongated jaw that gave her a masculine air. Her designer dress bespoke Jet Set, and Aldous saw a young man lying dead on a bed in a New York hotel room before she spoke.

"It's like this," she said baldly. "Before my father died, well, just minutes before he died, he made me promise to look after my brother, who's a year younger than I am, and he's always been a bit wild. Now, that's the worst form of blackmail – death-bed blackmail. My brother's my father's son – that's one thing. But I'm not my brother's keeper. And what's worse, he resents my interfering, my trying to look after him. You see," she said, appealing to Aldous, "There's nothing really I can do. So, he was with me in Marbella and in Montecarlo, for almost a year. He'd make trouble at parties – getting drunk or getting high on drugs. Too much of that and people start looking at you twice – you know? So, finally I told him to get lost, and I've heard not a word from him in almost year. Now, suddenly, I've got this feeling of real unease –"

"He's dead," said Aldous.

She slumped, her bare shoulders loosening as though screws had fallen out of them.

She finally got out, "Where?"

"He's lying on a bed in a flea bag hotel in New York. Overdose. He's been there twenty-four hours. In a couple of hours, someone will go knocking on the door – and, well, you know."

"Know!"

"The smell will alert them."

"What is the name of the hotel?"

"I can't see it. Go straight to the US consul, and explain. He'll make sure you are notified."

She wobbled to her feet, fumbled in her bag with nerveless fingers, and paid him.

* * *

The next visitor was an aging playboy of about fifty, Canadian, still handsome, athletic and trim, but his years showed in the dry wrinkles under his tan. He was nattily dressed, but he slumped into the chair.

"I guess my problem is that I'm bored. I've got what's called a good life, money no problem, but nowadays, I keep feeling fed up with everything. Mind you, I like it here, and I go to parties every night, and the beach every day. People like to sneer at parties, but I love them. But the truth is nothing seems to have much point, and what I want to know is where am I going? What's going to happen to me? Where's this all going to end up?"

Aldous said, "You've got two lovers, one of seventeen, the other eighteen. You three have group sex, and for you it's great. But you know they're interested only in the money, the restaurants, the parties. At the parties, you're scared someone will take them off you, but you've seen they always stay loyal. But they're young – and you're not. You see those young bodies and it gives you anguish. There's an Italian woman – ah – Charo, is that her name?"

"God, no!" he exploded. "She's forty-five. She's bossy. She's...!"

"She won't make you feel so old. She'll look after you, now that it's so important. She's got money, got class, is poised –"

"And she's forty-five," the man muttered. "I can see we're not on the same wavelength. Are you trying to tell me that's *she's* my future?"

"Something like that," Aldous said. "Your parties are very important. You need lots of people, to talk to them, to get around and socialise. That's what keeps you on an even keel, keeps you going. However, there's more in your future –"

Aldous paused, and the two men looked at each other for a beat.

"Years ago, you were thinking about going to India, to visit gurus there. For a whole year, you were toying with the idea."

"God, I'd completely forgotten that. That's old history. It'd never come into my mind since, what d'you think of that. You're telling me that's what I'm going to do?"

Aldous nodded.

"Can't believe it. Well, that gets rid of Charo!"

"I'm afraid she'll be going with you."

The man let out a sudden breath of air.

"And the guru's going to teach me to have no sex at all?"

"I don't know about that. There is a Yoga of Sex, you know. Depends on the gurus you see."

135

"I'm going to see more than one guru?"

"That's right. You have to contact the Indian Embassy to ask for a list of ashrams. Go to Madrid. personally. Don't do it by mail."

"At what age will I die?"

"I am not allowed to tell you that," said Aldous reprovingly. "You've got a long run yet."

The man paid him and left.

Gulliver sent, "Why don't they all ask when they will die?"

"Too scared. Too horrible. You couldn't live your life properly, knowing that."

"That man had another worldline open to him. Children with his nymphets."

"His life would be in an uproar. He's fifty, and never faced much responsibility. A violent wrench like that!" Aldous sent. "He's adapted to the jet set, to gurus, to socialising..."

* * *

His next client was a twenty four-year-old girl, wealthy, feminine, thin and frightened. She was French.

"I've been living for five years with a multimillionaire. He's Danish, he's forty-one. I don't have any money of my own. My mother has a shop in Pau, in the south of France. My husband, well, he's kept pretty busy. He often has to travel on business, leaving me here, or in Cannes, or in Copenhagen, where he has houses. Mainly I live here, because here there's lots of people and lots of parties. I get pretty lonely in Cannes and Copenhagen, although in Cannes I can go along to Montecarlo, where I know a lot of people. When my husband is here, he spends a lot of time on the phone, or at his computer screens – so –"

She took a deep breath

"I'm not unhappy, hut I'm not very happy either."

She sat in silence for a moment.

"Well, this friend of mine from Pau, Pierre, he came here on holiday. We saw each other and it was wonderful talking to him. He works for his father who's got a draper's. My husband was away, we started drinking – and, I'm afraid we ended up in bed. And, well, I'm afraid I'm pregnant. Pierre's back in France, and knows nothing. But my husband – well, he's not my husband – the Dane I'm living with – you see, well... he's sterile."

"And you want to know how will he react if he knows?"

"Oui."

Aldous sat for about two minutes.

"He wants to keep you, because you're so much younger than he is.

He's proud of you, and likes to show you off. You excite him, every time he sees you. He has never offered to marry you, because he feels he's sterile and too old. Now he will offer to marry you. He'll claim the girl as his own, and he'll be proud of her too. The baby girl will show he has a virility which in fact he does not have."

The Frenchwoman said doubtfully, "Are you sure of all this?"

"This is what will happen. You are young, very good-looking. You know how to dress, and you instinctively fit in to these high social circles. You know how to handle him, how to look after him. This is what will happen, because, after all is said and done, you've earned your place on your merits, it's not just something that has been handed to you, something that you're not really suited to. Because these are feelings you have, unfortunately, and they're not realistic, these feelings. You do fit in, and you're making him happy. You will have two more children, by artificial insemination, on his suggestion. His only fear will be that someone could find out that he is sterile. He must be able to feel that he can trust you completely."

She gave him a radiant smile, opened her handbag, and pulled out three ten thousand peseta notes, then impulsively pushed another note into his hand, which he accepted gracefully.

* * *

His next visitor was a middle-aged American.

The man sat down squarely on the chair, rubbing his fist with his open hand. He had a thin, taut face, was dressed casually and expensively, with a gold Rolex watch.

He gave Aldous a direct stare, and said, "I've got a problem, and I admit it. I'm aggressive, I get pissed off too easily. I dunno how I was born that way, but it sometimes screws things up, and that's what I've got on my mind right now."

Aldous said, "We're each born with a different character, but sometimes we lose sight of what we're really like, who we really are. And then, what happens, well, it just happens, but what matters is how we see it, the slant we give it. Your parents were aggressive and dominant. Your father built up a huge business, and he threw his weight around without quarter, and got away with it? Why? Because he was the boss, and he had to behave that way to protect himself, his business and his employees. And he *could* behave that way, because he had all that power behind him. Mind you, he'd come up the hard way, and earned every cent he had. Your mother moved into high society, on the back of all that money, and on the back of your father's position. She was successful as a society hostess because she was a mean in-fighter.

137

"Your parents were born that way, and you could say one was made for the other.

"You've got a completely different personality. Your parents pushed you into the business, and you hated it. You could have studied music. But you had to learn to be tough, play it their way, and when they died, you unloaded the business as fast as you knew how and kept the money.

"Today, you move in another world, but you still try to boss everyone. At the drop of a hat, you interpret what happens as an attack on yourself, or a threat. But that's not the way you are. Your parents have skewed you. And now you want to know about your possible marriage."

The man blinked. "Eh, yeah, that's what I came here for. Wow! "

"It's not going to work," Aldous said.

"That's what I was afraid of."

"You'll hound her, and she's going to walk out, after some months."

"Suppose I ought to see a shrink?"

Aldous said, "That's what is going to happen. You'll receive therapy for almost a year. Some months later, you'll meet the lady who will become your wife."

The man nodded dumbly, then grinned, and said, "Hey, you paint a rosy picture when you think about it. Am I going to learn to play the piano?" he quipped.

"It's not that rosy," smiled Aldous. "But you're going to enjoy life. After your marriage, you'll spend a lot of time down in the Caribbean."

Back home, after the evening meal, at 11 pm, Gulliver came out to Aldous, who was in a lounge chair beside the swimming pool.

Gulliver said, "Aldous, I've got a date. I need you to drive me."

"A date," cried Anna. "Who is she? Gulliver, you can't take Aldous. Three's a crowd! Don't worry about borrowing the car. It's yours! Where did you meet her?"

Gulliver said, "I need Aldous to show me the way."

"But if Aldous comes home with the car, how do you get back?"

"Not to worry," Gulliver told her airily.

"Ah! *She'll* drive you back. If she doesn't drive you straight to her

138

place, and then you find you can't get out again. Eh?" Anna smiled wickedly.

"A respectable old man like me! I'm not in any danger. Nothing to worry about."

"Hah! hah! This isn't the desert in the Australian Outback. This is the Marbella jungle."

Gulliver grinned at her affectionately.

"If I get into more than I can handle, I'll summon you."

"I can't wait to meet this demure creature."

In the car, Gulliver said, "Take the road to Fuengirola. We have to go to Alora, and then take the road across to Peñarrubia Ardales. On that road, we have to turn off."

"And this is a girl friend?" asked Aldous dubiously.

"People who want to meet me."

The road climbed up a river valley, the air getting cooler. At Alora, with the high country against the night sky, they turned left, and after a long stretch, Gulliver told him to watch for a dirt road leading north. They found it, and driving slowly, humped and jolted upward, crossing into one dip after another. Fifteen minutes later, Gulliver told him to stop the car, and they got out. Before them, high ridges stood against the sky, and in the small, shallow valley the air was a cool relief.

Aldous stared up at the stars, then around him, waiting for his eyes to adjust.

He saw orange and yellow lights approaching – a plane flying low? Then he saw a disc, the lights around its edge, and it came into towards them, then settled some fifty metres away. It stood about four meters high, and Aldous put it at about 60 metres across.

"Come", said Gulliver, and they walked across to it, picking their way carefully on the broken ground, feeling each step.

A rectangle of light opened in the side, and three figures stepped out, and walked towards them, shining a light on the ground. They came together on a flat, rocky outcrop.

The figure carrying the light set it on the ground, where it suddenly emitted a strong glow, showing the three figures clearly, and. lighting up

Aldous and Gulliver.

The three figures were slender, about five-foot six in height, Aldous guessed. They had long, thin necks, and oval, elongated heads, very bulbous towards the top, with huge, black, slanted eyes, and small mouths, but no nose.

They appeared to be naked, but perhaps wore a close-hugging garment the same colour as their heads. They were olive coloured, tending to green. They had no hair and no sexual organs.

Aldous heard Gulliver send, "Greetings."

The figure on the left, slightly taller than the other two, sent, "Greetings."

After a pause, it sent, "Who is this human?"

Gulliver sent, "He is my Guide and confidante here on earth."

"A human!"

"My Guide and confidante."

"He is a special human?"

"He is special. Indeed!"

"Where are you from?"

Gulliver projected, and Aldous suddenly saw an enormous space with thousands of lights scattered through it. One light blinked and expanded and contracted rapidly.

"Ah," sent the creature.

"That is the planet Xhemptuw, and I am called Zuxkirw, from that planet. Where are you from?"

Again, Aldous saw the enormous space with thousands of lights, one of which expanded and contracted while blinking.

"Ah!" said Gulliver. "This is a quadrant of the Milky Way we have never entered."

"This is the planet Betsab, and we are Betsabians. We have no names, but serial designations. You may call me *One*."

"Greetings, *One*. We are nine planets."

"All Xhemptuwians?"

"No. Each one is different. The oldest planet achieved technology half a million years ago. As each new planet was discovered, it was initiated into the higher science and technology. All are on the same level."

"You have come here to initiate humans in a technology half a million years old!"

"I doubt it. That is not within my writ. I have come to inspect and report. You have set up a robotic quarantine beyond the Oort Cloud."

"We have observed humans closely for thousands of years, but about fifty years ago, they exploded an atomic bomb. We carried out an intensive inspection with hundreds of craft. Humans are not of rational consciousness. They are intelligent killer animals. That we have found. We cannot allow them into the galaxy, into the Milky Way."

"They dispose only of chemical energy. There is no danger."

"We cannot guarantee the future."

"Why did not you vaporise them?"

"In our sacred Pyx lie the divine Mandates of the First Dimension. That can never be."

"We have the same Mandates. We sent craft to investigate your cordon beyond the Oort Cloud. They opened fire on us, and we had to deactivate them. We have reactivated them."

"Your craft are at a high level of development!"

"Our development greatly exceeds yours. We have a Confederation of Nine Planets. If you wish to join, may we send you an emissary?"

"Accepted. Yourself?"

"I have been nominated, and have accepted. Are you one planet alone?"

"We have colonised three other planets. Our four planets belong to a galactic Commonwealth."

"Of how many planets?"

"In the Milky Way, 17 planets in all. We occupy one half of the Milky Way. But the most advanced planet, which leads us, is in the Large Magellanic Cloud, with 13 other planets. The message your Confederation sent through our robots has been retransmitted to our principal planet in the Large Magellanic Cloud, and your emissary is expected."

"I will need a Guide."

The Betsabian gestured to the figure beside him. "This is *Two*, and he will guide you. Where is your craft?"

"Underwater, in Hudson Bay."

"Must it surface to take on our disc, or can our disc dock underwater?"

"Underwater. A robot will await you over Hudson Bay. I will not return immediately to my craft, because my work has not yet ended."

"How have you taken on human form? Have you killed...?"

"Never. I created this form from DNA."

"Ah!" came simultaneously from the Betsabians. "We do not have this level. Do your people wish to occupy this planet?"

"Our First Dimension mandates forbid that."

"Ah! Like us! Good! But we think that perhaps humans will build the Vtaksduym weapon, and destroy themselves."

Gulliver stared for more than a minute.

"Indeed. You are right. And if they survive, they will build the Zokvik..."

"Exactly," said *One*. "And they will *not* survive that weapon."

"They will not. They will destroy themselves."

"We have taken DNA of their flora, and will replant this planet. Then

141

we will occupy it. We will not reconstitute their fauna. Evolution has taken an incomprehensible course on this planet..."

"Indeed!"

After a minute, Gulliver asked, "Why do you keep jumping in and out of the Fourth Dimension, where human observers and human radar can register you?"

"Human brains cannot conceive of something appearing and then disappearing in thin air. Ergo, we don't exist. 'The witnesses are not reliable.'"

"Ah!"

"See what lengths you have gone to hide your presence. No one will know you have come. With ourselves, there are endless conjectures. We depend on discrediting the witnesses, and have done so. You don't have this problem."

"Indeed!

After a pause, Gulliver said, "You are welcome on my craft when you wish to go."

"Thank you. *Two* will see you soon and accompany you to the Large Magellanic Cloud."

They turned, and went back to their disc.

Gulliver and Aldous got back in the car. It would not start until the disc had risen, and raced swiftly to the north-east.

They drove back to the surfaced road.

Two kilometres along the road, Aldous stopped the car, got out and stood bent forward in an uncontrollable fit of shaking.

Gulliver said, "Your preconceptions have been smashed,. For humans, your preconceptions *are* yourselves, and when your preconceptions shatter, you are shattered. But nothing's changed. You aren't in danger – you are not going to be in danger in the years you have to live. Everything is the same for you."

Aldous caught control of himself, and mumbled, "I'm glimpsing worlds – I don't know whether I'll go mad. My mind's numb – I can't take it in."

"You can take it in and you will take it in. I said to them that you are

142

special, and you must think of yourself as special."

Aldous began to laugh, and felt better.

He said, "I don't want to feel special. I want to feel sane again."

"You are sane," said Gulliver comfortably. "Come on, man. Weren't you surprised to see that they were bipedal?"

"You've got me thinking like you. I *was* surprised."

"I probed, and found that one other planet in their Commonwealth within the Milky Way is also bipedal – the inhabitants, I mean."

"How long have they been advanced, I wonder?"

"I found that out too," said Gulliver smugly. "About 25,000 years."

"Isn't that long enough to discover everything you already know?"

"No, not enough. The oldest planet in the Commonwealth, in the Magellanic Cloud, is about 170,000 years. But it depends on brilliance. Our third planet, in our Confederation, the inhabitants are of a brilliance beyond all compare. And when the intelligences from different planets work together, the results stagger you."

They drove down towards the coast.

Gulliver settled back in his seat and groaned, "Now I have to go to the Great Magellanic Cloud."

Aldous sympathised, "There's no rest for the wicked."

Gulliver said, "It's wicked all right."

Next morning, they had a late breakfast at a cafe, sitting at outside tables in the shade, facing the sea. It was hot, and they drank iced coffee.

Aldous read the newspapers, then pushed them aside impatiently.

"For the first time in the history of the Galaxy, representatives from the Confederation meet people from the Commonwealth of Planets, and not a word in the Press. If you want to know what's really going on, you're wasting your time with TV and newspapers."

Gulliver said approvingly, "You're widening your viewpoints. You can't keep your nose down on the surface of the earth, my dear Aldous, you cannot."

Then he said, "Isn't it hot! Let's get down on the beach and join the others."

They paid, picked up their beach bags, and crossed the Promenade to the beach.

* * *

After they had gone in the sea, and had a shower on the beach, they stretched out on their beach towels. Carla said, "Daddy, I keep remembering myself in another place, with another name. It was horrible. I was in Sevilla, but hundreds of years ago. Everyone was dressed the way they are shown in our history books. They were looking for me – they were going to burn me as a witch. I dressed in a man's clothes – in brown homespun, and rode a donkey to Cordoba. I cut my hair and put on a hat. It was so frightening. I had gold coins, and I bought clothes to dress as a gypsy fortune-teller, and made money telling fortunes. No one could catch me because no one knew who I was. At the market one day, I saw a rich lady, and I told her she was going to face three dangers – that in a few minutes, someone would cut her purse; that at the end of the street a carriage would run her down: and that if she went the next day to a village she wanted to go to, she would die of fever. She had a guard with her, so she warned the guard, and he caught the cutpurse. At the end of the street, she stepped into a doorway, and a carriage swung around so close it tore her dress. So she told me, 'I am not going to that village, tomorrow', and I said, 'Take me on as your maid and companion,' and she thought about it, and took me to her home, where I lived for five years, till I married.

"It's not a dream, because I can see it all and feel it when I'm awake. It's so frightening. What's the matter with me?"

Aldous explained gently, "You have reincarnated. That is, you have lived before, and now you have been reborn as my daughter – you have reincarnated as my daughter. All this is absolutely real and true. It happened to you in that life. Very few people can remember earlier lives, but you are psychic."

"And what about you, daddy?"

"I was a Western Highlander. Thousands of those people have second-sight, as they call it. I lived near Ullapool, and I was a fisherman. We lived in a low, grey, stone cottage, with turf on the roof and life was very hard. I chose to be reborn in London, so I could help people by giving them Readings."

"Why didn't you give Readings in the Western Highlands?"

"Because there they never talk about the second-sight. Everyone knows, but they don't speak of it. Thousands of people there have it. It runs in families."

Carla sat lost in thought.

She turned to her brother. "Jorge, what do you remember?"

144

"I was an astronomer in America. Got killed in a car accident."

He glowered at Gulliver.

"I'm not going to be an astronomer this time. You're searching the heavens, but you don't see what really matters. It's like having a telescope on the Moon and looking at Washington through it. Maybe you see all those buildings, but you don't know what's going on inside."

He glared at Gulliver, who smiled at him sunnily.

Gulliver asked, "What *do* you want to do, then?"

"Wanna be a physicist," the boy muttered.

Anna asked Aldous, "What was I in my last reincarnation? Is this really serious?"

"It's serious all right," Aldous assured her. "In your last reincarnation, you lived in London, married to a bank employee. You had two children, and lived a life of slow monotony. You were French, and had married this Englishman, who would come home late, because he frequented the street women of Victorian London. Your father was a wheelwright, in the north of France, and he adored you, his daughter. He had a small workshop, employing four men, to build wooden farm carts. So you all planned your escape.

"Your father sold his business, and he and your mother moved to the south of France, to Pélissanne, in Provence, where he opened another workshop. Your parents changed their name. Your mother came to London, and one morning, you left a letter for your husband, and with your children took the train to catch the ferry to France. The children were told they had a new surname because they were in a new country. Your husband searched for his children, but you had all disappeared into the air. He hired detectives, but they never found you. You and your father were close, and your father would do anything for you."

Anna said sceptically, "And I was happy for ever after?"

"Yes, it was much better than before. You had a discreet liaison with a landowner, who helped your purse, you had sunlight, red and white wine, provençal food, loving parents, people to talk to... in London, you were inhumanly lonely."

* * *

A tall, heavily-built American walked over to them. He wore swimming trunks, and had the beginnings of flab around his middle, but muscle showed on his arms and chest.

He said, "Hi! I couldn't help hearing you speak English. You from the States?"

"I'm from Toronto," said Aldous.

145

"I've been in Australia," offered Gulliver.

"This is my first trip to visit the famous Med. There's a group of us, down there in Marbella. I thought I'd do some exploring on my own, and here I am! We did the French Riviera, then headed down the Spanish coast. That Riviera is world famous, and what a dump! And the Spanish coast! What an eyesore! Goddam ramshackle, jerry-built tower blocks. Arabs everywhere! Dirt and dust, noise —you'd think this was New York. Who invented all this crap of the romantic Med, the historic Med, 'colourful' Spain – Jeez!

What'ya think of this after Toronto? A real pain, eh?"

"Well, I live here," said Aidous.

Anna said, "I'm his wife. *I* live here with the children. *He* comes and goes."

Aldous said, "You don't really see the buildings when you get used to living here."

"So what's it got?"

"It's another way of living. The tourist never gets to see that. Back in Toronto the bottom line's money... here, money's sorta important but there're other things."

The American sat down, shook his head, and said, "Well, if money's not important to you, I guess..."

Gulliver laughed. "Aldous' love of money is awesome."

"Ah! Gotcha!" cried the American.

Aldous said, "Here they're more sociable... more hospitable... I dunno..."

Gulliver said unhelpfully, "They're hospitable and sociable in Australia – but Australia's not Europe."

"I don't know what it is, "Aldous admitted.

"It better be pretty good," said the American grimly. "Because just to look at it, it's lousy!"

"There's a lot of culture," suggested Gulliver mildly.

"Come on!" laughed the American. "Don't give me that line!"

That afternoon, in Aldous' office in Marbella, the first visitor was a plump Spaniard, about forty-five, with worry lines in his forehead, his cheeks drawn and sagging. He was perspiring in the heat, and sat thankfully in the chair.

"Would you like something to drink?"

"Only make me perspire more, but many thanks," he said in a tired voice, despondently,

"Well," he said, despondently, "The situation is this. I'm from up north, from Barcelona. I've worked all my life in a big bank. For the last seven years, I dealt directly with the public – enquiries, complaints, you know. The bank has merged with another giant bank, and when giants get together, we little men get squashed. They retrenched – about two thousand people, here in Spain and abroad. To find a job at my age! I'm twenty years away from a pension, so how do I find work? I've been sending in replies to every ad in sight, and I'm wasting my time."

His mouth twitched, as he got control of himself.

Aldous said, "Years ago, you studied English. You visited England twice on holidays. Now you have to study English ever day, and practise talking. You are down here with your parents, so you can stop here, and practise talking with tourists. But you must find yourself a private teacher. In six months, you will return to Barcelona. Catalonia has a very strong export sector. You will answer ads for representatives to be trained in the export firms – go to all the interviews to get practice in interviewing. Go to *all* the interviews. After two and half months, a firm will take you on, at a very low salary, because they will be training you. You will accept that salary. After a year, they will send you abroad, and after three months of travelling, when they see that you are successful, they will quadruple your salary. And you will get commissions."

The man stared at him speechlessly.

"That's too good to be true. But you know all about me! You must be speaking the truth. Good, I'm going to do that."

He took out 30,000 pesetas, and Aldous said brusquely, "There's no charge." He got up and escorted that man to the door, then smiled. "I'm not going to wish you good luck, because you're going to be all right."

* * *

She wore a simple, expensive dress. Her body was small, finely-built and sexy, but her very long, lanky legs made her look very tall. Her face showed classical bones, with pouting lips. She looked tough and alert.

"I do travel videos for television. Trouble is, to place them. I've broken into one Spanish and one Portuguese television station, but it's tough. The big money is in the States, but if I could get into British, French or German channels, I'd be halfway home. I live in Marbella because I like partying with these people. The Arabs also give me work, doing professional family videos,

147

and they pay high. They've got these tremendous houses in Marbella, and they like videos of their homes – but done professionally.

"Well, I've met this guy, he's a Yank, and he's a high-up in one of the main U.S. chains. So, he's going to the Caribbean, and wants me to go with him. He's being really urgent about getting into my panties, and I've been holding off. Question is, will he help me place my videos in his chain, because then I've made it? And I'll get a trip to the Caribbean. But if I deliver him my fair white body, then that's it. I've got no more cards to play."

Aldous said, "He's already decided that your videos will go. He wants them. But he's holding out because he wants to take you to bed. Whether you go to bed or not, he'll finally buy your stuff. If you go to the Caribbean with him, he'll sign you a contract."

"And do you suppose he wants to marry me?"

"He hasn't even thought of it. He is not the man you are going to marry. The man you *will* marry, will find out about this Caribbean trip and he'll have a hard time forgiving you."

"I'm going to marry someone like that! He doesn't have to forgive anything I did before I met him and married him!"

"He's not that sort of person."

"Who is he?"

"You'll meet him in a year and half's time. You'll get married three months later."

"But who is he?"

"Don't ask. Just enjoy everything as it happens."

"Well, I don't know what I'm going to do. What interests me now is the Caribbean. If my Yank has got the patience, I'll shoot some film. Hey, I might even put him in the shots. He might go for that."

"He will," Aldous assured her. "You'll find him photogenic, and you'll make his face familiar to millions. He'll love you for that."

She said shrewdly, "And my future husband is going to see this feature."

Aldous nodded.

She opened an expensive handbag, and paid him.

* * *

Aldous recognised his next visitor. He was a famous actor. He gave Aldous a dazzling smile, sauntered in, and sat down comfortably, crossing his legs but jiggling his foot.

Aldous said, "I've seen some of your films. Like them very much."

"Thanks," the actor said lazily. "But have you seen scenes where I'm in the mountains, or high up inside an abandoned factory, or on a roof forty

148

stories high, or on a high balcony outside a window..."

Aldous nodded.

"Well, I should do those shots myself. No big deal. But mostly, we have to put in a double, and that pisses off the studio. They can't understand for the life of them why I can't drive up a mountainside, get out and walk around."

Aldous held up his hand, and sat for four minutes. "Your last reincarnation was six thousand years ago. You were climbing in the French Alps, pursued by about a dozen men. You wore a long grass cape... it was winter... you had huge gumboots made of hide and packed with grass... you carried a spear and stone knife ...

Aldous moved his chair.

"I am now going to hypnotise you... you are relaxing... relaxing... relaxing... going deeper – and deeper – and down, down, down... you are in the French Alps six thousand years ago, in winter..."

The actor writhed in his chair, his face contorted, perspiration staining his shirt.

"They're chasing me! – my boots keep slipping – they're catching up – I am climbing icy rocks beside a deep gorge – I have to cross patches of ice and I can't get purchase – I'm down on my hands and knees – I'm back on rock – there's a bridge down in the gorge, two tree trunks – I'll cross and tip the trunks into the gorge – I've got down to the bridge – I'm crossing – a spear hits me in the middle of the back, like fire – I've gone over – I'm falling onto the rocks at the bottom of the gorge –"

"Relax!" commanded Aldous. "You're lying comfortable and relaxed in the bottom of the gorge now, you will slowly awake, and you will remember this. You are slowly awakening. I'm going to count to ten, and when I say ten, you will awake, perfectly relaxed, unafraid, and you will remember this."

Aldous counted to ten. The actor sighed, and sat back in the chair.

"My God," he said. "What a nightmare!"

"It was six thousand years ago," Aldous reminded him.

"My, how time passes," quipped the actor.

Then he said, "This can't be true. You put the idea into my head."

"I promise you, this really happened."

"I don't believe in this reincarnation stuff. There's no proof that this isn't just a product of my imagination."

Aldous heard Gulliver's voice. "Put him under, again."

Aldous said, "I'm going to hypnotise you again."

In five minutes, the actor was under.

Gulliver sent, "Tell him to take off all his clothes."

"Take off all your clothes. Undress."

The actor stripped naked.

Aldous heard Gulliver sending to the actor, "You are going back in

149

time, a thousand years, two thousand, three – five – six. You are climbing down to the bridge..."

The actor gasped and rocked in his chair.

"You are close to the bridge – now come, back to the present!"

Aldous saw opaque ripples of white-greyish light, and the actor stood before him, dressed in hides, with bulky hide boots, and a long woven grass cape.

"Awake!" commanded Gulliver.

The actor looked about him, dazedly, then down at his dress.

"My God," he whispered. He touched the cape, bent down and felt the wet boots. He ran his hands up and down his hide jacket and trousers, and found a stone knife.

He said reluctantly, "It looks as though I left my spear behind. Studio costuming never had anything like this..."

"You may care to get back into twentieth century attire," grinned Aldous, turning his back and looking out of the window.

After he was dressed, the actor asked, "Can I take this outfit?"

Aldous nodded. "You may care to check with a museum, for radioactive carbon dating."

"That's a damned good idea... or is it? If they ask me how I got it, and I tell them, they'll lock me in a loony-bin and lose the key. Jeez! Do you have bags, or wrapping paper? I'll have to wear the cape over my shoulders – in this heat!"

"People are going to look at you."

"That's my problem always – to make 'em look at me! Except they won't be paying any tickets."

He undid a pouch he wore around his waist, and paid Aldous.

Aldous showed him to the door, and the actor shook hands warmly.

"Take it from me, you orta be in show biz!"

* * *

His next visitor was in her late twenties, plump, sexy, stylish. She had spent a fortune on her simple dress, and her face was deceptively girlish and appealing.

"I've been knocked up," she said baldly. "He's great in bed, he's great for a good time, he's poised and smooth at parties. To go to a restaurant with – there's no one better. But he's not superficial. He's moody, he's complex, he's hard to understand. Well, he's intriguing in a way, you get what I mean? I'm never bored because I'm never sure what's going on in that head of his. He keeps doing and saying unexpected things. It's never been a balanced relationship, if you get my drift. Most girls want comfort and security, but I

150

get a kick out of him. I keep thinking I've got him figured, and then I get a surprise. We women like to think we can read men like a book, but about the only thing I can read with him is his cock. I generally know at what stage it's at."

"And he's boyish," murmured Aldous. "You feel a bit motherly towards him."

"That's part of his charm. Exactly."

"He's boyish, because he's immature as hell. He's unpredictable because he's a little boy who wants all his own way. The woman before you, she got breast cancer, and he dumped her. She went back to the States for the operation."

"I thought they had a tiff..."

"Before that, his girlfriend had to have a gall bladder op. He dropped her like a hot brick."

"So, you know what I've come to ask. Is he going to want our baby and will he marry me?"

"You won't see him for dust. But if you take him to court, and use DNA testing, you'll take him for a fortune. Yet you've got your own money."

"How much is a court going to award for upkeep against a multi-millionaire father?"

"Yearly payments can be made into a Trust for when the girl is twenty-one."

"A girl!"

"You ask the court, and they'll probably grant it."

"I don't know that I want to."

"I know you don't," said Aldous.

"What sort of girl will she be when she grows up?"

"Disappointing. Mixed-up. Complicated and unhappy. No matter how you rear a child, there are always the genes."

He paused. "But she'll make a good marriage, and straighten out quite a bit."

"Well, that's it, I guess."

She opened her handbag, and took out the money.

Aldous sent to Gulliver, "I knew what was going to happen. You can't change what's going to happen."

He took her to the door, breathing in her heady perfume.

On the drive back to Torre Real, Gulliver said, "We have to go to London. I can't wait any longer."

"We'll be arrested! When they see us at Heathrow Airport, my God! They'll have a tank waiting for us!"

"Why a tank?"

"They'll figure it's too heavy to shift to Alaska," said Aldous morosely.

"Those gentlemen are home from Alaska, and our names are subject to much discussion. But they can't arrest us, because we have done nothing. As the Prime Minister pointed out, there have been cases of people walking across a field and vanishing in the blink of an eye. No one accused the farmer. It was recognised that a time or space warp had formed inside that field and – poof! That person stepped into it."

"Will they be watching us?"

"I'm going to put a mental block on everyone who knows about us. They won't be able to speak of it. Not a word. So nothing will be done. Besides, imagine, they invite you to Scotland Yard, to help them with their inquiries, and you start sending the people there all over the globe. No, the mental block will do. When we get to the house, I'll phone to make reservations for tomorrow."

* * *

At home, they sat outside beside the swimming pool. Aldous went in, changed into his swimming trunks, came out and plunged into the pool. He swam some lengths, then floated on his back, looking at the sky.

Jorge came out, sat by the pool, and looking at Gulliver, said, "I want to go back with you. I can get a much better education on your planet."

Aldous convulsed, and nearly swallowed water. He floundered to the edge, and climbed out.

"What planet?" he blustered.

"Beyond the stars."

Aldous stared.

"You can't disappear from earth," he said reasonably. "We'd have police all over, looking for you. Your mother would think you were dead, and

152

go mad."

"I'll leave a note to say I'm running away."

"Can you imagine the suffering that is going to cause her!"

"Gulliver can put a mental block on her."

The two men sat and considered him in thoughtful silence.

Gulliver said, "I'm not going straight back home. I've got to go to the Large Magellanic Cloud first."

"I know, and I want to go there too."

The two men sat in silence.

After some minutes, Gulliver said, "Jorge, you'll come back to earth with knowledge thousands of years in advance of what they have here. It'll be useless. You won't get published. You have to suffer peer reviews. There's so much in-fighting and jealousy among scientists, such a struggle for funding, it's a wonder any science gets done at all. Jorge, imagine a forty-storey building. *You* have all the bricks. But you can't place the bricks on the fortieth-story, when they are laying the first-storey courses. You can lay bricks only on the last course – way down on the first-storey. If you do get published, you'll he considered a pure scientist – but with no practical application in sight."

Jorge said, "I'd come back only for the lifetimes of mum and dad. When they die, I want to go back to your planet. When mankind is wiped out, I can return and begin repopulating the earth. You will be able to genetically modify my brain so we'll no longer be animals."

"Precocious child," said Gulliver, admiringly.

"It's clear he's my offspring," Aldous noted modestly.

"Jorge, listen," said Gulliver. "Back on my planet, we'll have to preserve your body, but your mind will have to move to one of our bodies. Four legs, four arms, and as ugly as sin by your earthly standards. How do like that? You'll hate it."

"No problem," said Jorge brashly. "I've thought of that already."

Gulliver breathed deeply.

"So you propose that the new human race will be your clones?"

"No, we're going to have company."

Gulliver paused, looking at him steadily.

"Indeed, we will."

"What's going on?" demanded Aldous, anxiously.

Jorge said, "Dad, you're about to get a phone call."

Aldous looked at him stupidly, then concentrated in silence.

"Oh my God!" he said.

"All your little chickens coming home to roost, daddy," said Jorge.

Gulliver said, "Jorge, when we get to the planet in the Large Magellanic Cloud, we don't know what the gravity will be. We may have to stay on board our space craft, protected by our Dark Energy screen, and communicate by

153

video screens. Or we may be able to go outside, but the atmosphere may attack my skin, so we'll have to go in a sort of sphere, and communicate through windows. Or the atmosphere may be neutral, but you can't breathe it. So you have to wear a breathing helmet, and to do that, you must be dressed in a suit to fix the helmet to. Any of these things can happen. Don't you think you'd be happier here, living normally and going to the beach?"

"I don't have any problem with those conditions."

They heard the phone ring in the house.

Aldous sighed. "I'm the one with the problems."

He walked towards the patio door, when the maid came out and said, "The phone for you, sir."

* * *

He picked up the phone, and said, "Annika!"

His daughter said, "Aren't you clever! You knew it was me before I spoke, Have I made you happy?"

"Very."

"I'm flying from Gothenburg tomorrow morning and I'll be in Malaga at eleven o'clock. Will you come and meet me?"

"Annika, I'm here with my brother. Would you mind pretending you are his daughter – my niece? You will appreciate the situation here, with Anna."

"No problem. You are leaving for London at two o'clock, and I've got an English visa. Would you book me onto your flight?"

Aldous was nonplussed.

"I can't wait to meet your brother, Gulliver. Some brother, eh?"

"We'll book the flight."

He hung up, and turned around to see Jorge and Gulliver standing behind him. They laughed at him.

Gulliver said, "Give me the phone. I've got to make that booking."

* * *

Jorge said, "I'm going to get mummy. Gulliver, can you put the mental block on her?"

The boy walked upstairs to where his mother was working at a linen cupboard, beside the bedrooms.

"Mummy, could you come downstairs?"

She looked at him glassy-eyed, and said mechanically, "Yes, dear."

Outside, they sat around the swimming-pool.

154

Jorge said unsteadily, "Mummy, Gulliver is not really Aldous' brother. He had come from beyond the stars, and now I am going with him, for about five years, to be educated. on another planet."

Aldous said, "You'll have to tell everyone that he has gone to a Catholic College in Britain. For five years, you will have to leave Torre Real in summer, and take your holidays where nobody knows you. We will say that Jorge has joined us there for summer."

Anna said mechanically, "Yes, dear. That's a very good idea. I am so happy for Jorge."

"I'll be all right, mummy. Gulliver will look after me."

"Gulliver will look after you."

Gulliver said, "Now we will take Jorge with us to London. Will you pack clothes for him?"

"I shall," said Anna.

"We'll leave about nine o'clock tomorrow morning," Aldous said.

Anna said, "I'll finish with the linen cupboard and then I'll pack his things."

She looked at them glassily.

Gulliver told her, "You will now relax, and you will look perfectly normal. Your face will wear a normal, tranquil expression."

She got to her feet and went back to the house.

Aldous turned to Gulliver. "Annika's mother is Maj-Britt."

"I will do the same to her. You must arrange for their summer holidays, so Annika's absence isn't noticed. Aldous, please concentrate on Maj-Britt, and on your house in Gothenburg, to guide me in. Ah! Or she might be at Amås, is it?"

Aldous stared at the grass, and centred his mind.

At Malaga airport, Annika came towards them, tall and willowy, sashaying and euphoric. She stopped before Jorge, and said, "Hello, brother dear. I didn't realise you were so small —"

"And I didn't realise you were skin and bone. Hungry days up where you come from?"

Annika tried to approach her father coolly, a young grown-up.

Suddenly, she cried and ran to him, wrapping her arms around him. They embraced, Annika incoherent. Then she collected herself, and shook hands with Guiliver. She tried to look seductive.

"I'm coming with you and Jorge. Tell me I can come! I can, can't I?"

Gulliver looked at her with resignation.

"Annika, can you seriously contemplate inhabiting the body of a huge spider-like animal?"

She said solemnly, "I know all about that. I got it all from your minds. I've worked through that problem, and disposed of my inhibitions and preconceptions."

"You have, have you?" remarked Gulliver drily. "Aren't you proud of your young beauty – don't you like human males ogling you?"

"That belongs to an earlier, immature stage of my development. Now my gaze is fixed on the heavens."

"On the heavens," echoed Jorge.

"Like you yourself," Annika smiled sweetly. "Little *jordnöt*."

Annika took Gulliver's arm. "You will be a darling, won't you, and set up a mental block in mummy's mind. You will, promise me."

Gulliver sighed.

"You'll see, you'll be ever so happy to have me with you."

"You and Jorge," corrected Gulliver.

"You'll never be sorry. It'll be a wonderful experience."

"It'll be an experience," agreed Gulliver.

"So it's agreed!"

He raised his hands helplessly.

"We'll see. Now we have to wait for the London plane. Let's find a sidewalk cafe. They're one of this planet's best features."

At Heathrow, they walked up to Passport Control, Aldous, Gulliver and Jorge stony-faced, Annika giggling. The man looked at Aldous' passport, pressed a button, and woodenly passed him on. He noted the names of the other three.

* * *

When they got out of the taxi, in front of Aldous' flat, they saw an unmarked police car.

Annika begged Gulliver, 'Please, send them to Australia. I'm reading their thoughts. You could stand them on their heads."

Jorge said, "Please, do! I have to see this to believe it."

"How do you know all about this?" growled Gulliver.

"Reading daddy's mind," they chorused together.

"Cease now this heedless levity," intoned Aldous. "Begone this frivolity."

Inside the flat, they dropped their luggage thankfully.

Aldous said, "This used to be my father's flat, and, thankfully, it has five bedrooms. My brothers and I have equal ownership. As they used it with their families, all the bedrooms have beds, and there's plenty of linen and blankets. I'm going to show you two kids your rooms, and where the linen is. Annika, you'll probably need only one blanket, of cotton, but Jorge you may need a light woollen blanket. Come on, and bring your suitcase."

* * *

They went for a walk, sightseeing. In Trafalgar Square, Gulliver said, "I'm going to be very busy in the Library." He smiled. "Studying your human brain."

"What for?" demanded Annika.

157

"To see what's to be done." Gulliver stared up at the metal lion.

"Why did you come here?" asked Jorge.

"To see whether we will advance you, your technology and your science by 3,000 years, in the first instance."

"But I thought we are going to wipe ourselves out with super weapons."

"Humanity will, if they are not advanced."

"So you will advance us?"

"Not necessarily. It might be better to let humanity wipe itself out."

"But that would be inhuman!" cried Annika.

They strolled across Trafalgar Square.

"It would be inhuman for the humans, but possibly a very good thing for everyone else. You know that you kill dangerous life forms. You kill bacteria and virus all the time. You try to stop them from getting a foothold – by washing your hands, by scouring or disinfecting." He said soothingly, "I don't know what I'm going to do. I have to study your human brain. On the face of it, your behaviour is atrocious. Possibly, something can be done. I don't know yet. I have to find out and send a report. This very Square – who in the Galaxy would make a Square a monument to a slaughter! I have to find the reason, and find whether you can be changed or not."

"You could change us!"

"We have a Sacred Pyx holding the Codex from the First Dimension. A race can change itself, can alter its own evolution. We cannot."

"Do you suppose other Aliens have come here?"

"I am very puzzled about that. You have been sending out electronic signals for 75 years, so perhaps others have caught them. Aliens have come from the Betsab planet. They belong to a Commonwealth, and that's where we're going first – to the head planet of that Commonwealth."

"And they won't help us?"

"They're terrified of you. They plan to occupy this planet after your self-extermination, so when you come back, you will share it with them. Without them, possibly you could not survive to rebuild your race."

"But you *will* modify our brains, when we get to your planet?" asked Jorge.

Three men passing them stopped dead, turned around and stared at them speechlessly.

"That is *the* big question," said Gulliver, pressing his lips together. "What we can't do with a whole race on a planetary surface, we may be able to do with two specimens off-planet. The Sacred Pyx will be opened and there will be much studying of the Codex."

"We're not specimens," said Annika spiritedly. "I'm *Annika*, and that's *Georgay*."

"'*Horhay*', is how you pronounce it," snapped Jorge.

158

Gulliver looked at them fondly.

"My repentant apologies," he said. "Well, coming back to Aliens. My Confederation, I imagine, has been as surprised as I have to find this Commonwealth with which we had never had contact. It is also possible that there are individual planets out there that are well advanced, and never emitted electronic signals. They went directly to the higher technologies. Or there could be yet another group of planets. So any of these Aliens could have come here in the last 75years, or even in a more remote past. If they have come in the last 75 years, it is curious that they are ignoring you. They may have seen you as threatening, and decided to return at a future date. They don't appear to have established surveillance. Of course, we must consider the possibility that their planets lie quite near and that they are not travelling through the Fourth Dimension – that they have not advanced that far. But if they lie within twenty light years from here, I'm sure we would have stumbled across them by accident.

"If they *are* Aliens who travel through the Fourth, which is much more likely, most definitely they did not like what they found here. They made no contact, and I suppose that in some years they'll be back again to make sure you are not ready to venture into space. I suppose they would stop you from doing so. Of course, they might find the Betsabian Cordon Sanitaire of robot ships, and then try to contact Betsab.

"It appears to me that in savagery, the Earth is alone. If another planet suffered maverick evolution as this planet has, and had advanced technology, they would come and wipe you out. But no planet has ever tried attacking us on Xhemtuw, obliging us to vaporise them."

They had walked down Whitehall.

"You see, the British Prime Minister's residence in Downing St is cordoned off. We can't go there! On the face of it, there is nothing at all to be done when you see something like that Prime Minister's residence, but allow the race to exterminate itself as fast as possible. Such a race has to disappear. Quickly! The residence cordoned off! A Prime Minister should be leading you to higher ground!"

They headed for Westminster Bridge.

"What you young people must never lose sight of is that life in this Dimension, in this Universe you see around you, is like going to the cinema, or to the theatre. You leave the First Dimension for new and strange experiences, new sights – for *change*! The First Dimension is unchanging. But here on Earth, the cinema is showing a horror film, a terror film. It's a prison, a hellhole, a sink of punishment and suffering, and that is the fault of evolution. Life was perhaps so precarious, so threatened, that evolution lost sight of everything in its goal for simple, savage survival. I *don't* know. Nothing has prepared me for this. The whole thing is unimaginable – is weird. A weird, impossible nightmare, I find it."

On the bridge, they looked at the Thames.

Gulliver drew a heavy breath.

"Well, that's why they sent Zuxkirw. To find out what is what, and why." He rubbed his hands over his face.

Jorge said, "That's your real name? I like Gulliver better. And you are really on your Gulliver's Travels, aren't you?"

"Nothing compared to the Gulliver's Travels awaiting you two," he grinned.

They stared at the Houses of Parliament, then walked back, towards St. James Park.

Annika said, "Isn't it funny that no one could believe an alien was walking around here."

"That's easy," said Aldous heavily. "We tend to believe that whatever level we're at is it. We can't really imagine what's coming. Last century, with the steam trains, who got impatient thinking about the big passenger jets? Babbage, was it? – he built a mechanical computer, but no one imagined an electronic computer. On other planets, they are so advanced, people here can't begin to imagine how. But if we grant they are a hundred thousand years ahead, of course they'll come here and walk around without our knowing it."

"The Prime Minister didn't know who walked past Downing Street," laughed Jorge, delighted.

Jorge added, as they approached St. James Square, "Daddy, to keep up Gulliver's disguise, why don't we all have an ice-cream?"

"Such concern!" said Aldous, shaking his head. "First, we have to find somewhere selling ice-cream."

"Well, we're on the right planet," said Gulliver. "They don't sell it anywhere else in the Galaxy – to my knowledge. And my knowledge is taking some knocks!"

* * *

Next morning, Annika and Jorge left with Gulliver, the two youngsters to explore London.

At half-past-ten, Aldous had his first visit, a young man about twenty-two, thin, with a pointed face and wispy beard, small eyes and a resigned twist to his mouth.

He sat with a small gesture, and told Aldous, "I'm a Drama student. I've finished the course, and have been looking for an opening for five months. In the mornings, I drive a milk truck, starting out at five o'clock and finishing about nine. In the evenings, I work in a bar from four to eight, so that pays for my upkeep. But I've got to face it, I've got an unprepossessing face – I look nondescript and would make a great spy. I could go unnoticed anywhere. So can you help me? Have I been a bloody fool, going into Drama, looking the way I do?"

Aldous regarded him thoughtfully, then raised his hand. He sat for about six minutes, and then said, "I see you in a play in Manchester, in the next few weeks. Something about an unemployed family... I can't see the details yet. I'm trying to see the name –"

"I know!" said the young man triumphantly. "You're telling me I should go up to Manchester to audition for it?"

He named the play, and the man who was putting it on.

Aldous raised his hand, and sat for a couple of minutes.

"Yes. That is the one. Those are the names."

He sat in stillness again.

Then he said, "I see you in a film – a Hollywood-British production. The main character is a woman – yes – a beautiful woman – ah, she's fleeing – she escapes to Britain – ah – er – she's in a hotel, where you're staying – she knocks on your door, you hide her – er, um – ah – you come up with this original idea to extricate her – you look pretty hopeless, but you come through, to the surprise of the audience. It's a good ploy – no one expects anything of you..."

Aldous stopped, and looked at him.

"There's a booking agent you have to go to after Manchester is finished."

He wrote down a name on a pad, and tore off the sheet.

The student looked at it.

"I know who that is!"

He shook his head. "But films! My passion is the theatre. I want to devote my life to Art. You mightn't be able to understand, but for me, Art is all."

"Driving a milk cart ain't Art," Aldous reproved him.

Aldous did not charge him.

* * *

161

The man was in his early forties.

He was plump, well-dressed, with a small nose and large eyes, that looked out appealingly from his face. His blonde hair was rumpled.

"I've been divorced about a year. I've got four kids, the eldest is eleven."

He crossed his legs, then uncrossed them. He crossed them again, and caught his knee with his hands, leaning forward.

"Well, I worked for a big computer company, and had to travel a lot, demonstrating mainly, to sell big mainframes. The wife got fed-up, and divorced me."

Aldous nodded.

"Well, I want to stay close to my kids, so I talked to the company, and they found another job for me, which keeps me in London. Suppose I should have done something like that before, hut you know how it is, wise after the event. Mind you, my wife's a Londoner, and that's another thing I had never realised. British women make awful wives, you know?"

Aldous nodded sympathetically, and said nothing.

"I've met this Hindu graduate, and – well, it's another world. But she's got a married sister with a hotel-restaurant, up in Scotland, in the Highlands, on the coast. The sister has arranged for members of her family to immigrate and join her up there. So, this Indian girl I'm in love with wants to go up there to be with all the family – her parents are coming, and another brother who's married with children. My fiancée graduated in electronics and she does software, so she can work from home up there. It won't matter she's got clients in England – she can always travel back and forth. And she's sure to get work in Scotland. She's got it all worked out.

"Except, I can't leave my company, and above all, I'm not going to leave my kids. I want to stay close to them, and see them as often as I can."

Aldous said, "You've had a complete change of heart about your children, and now you're trying to make amends."

The other said eagerly, "That's right. That's it exactly. But what is my fiancée going to do?"

"She's jealous of your feelings towards your children. She's going to bring every ounce of pressure to bear on you that she can. She will say goodbye to you, and go up to Scotland, to see her family. She will stay there for three weeks, ringing you and begging you to come, warning you that she is not coming back. She will tell you she has found a house for you both.

"At the end of three weeks, she will come back, and go on working in London as before. Next year, you will marry. You will try to involve her with your children, and you'll succeed. She's going to slowly grow fond of them – slowly – but she will."

The man was clasping and unclasping his fingers. There were beads of

162

perspiration on his face.

"Thank you, indeed, thank you," he said with a strained voice.

He pulled out his wallet from his breast pocket, and pressed the bank notes into Aldous' hand. Aldous probed swiftly. The notes were not marked.

At the door, the man impulsively shook Aldous' hand, holding his elbow with the other hand.

* * *

Gulliver didn't come home for lunch. Annika and Jorge were full of their morning's walk. They had taken the Underground to Oxford St, and after looking at the shops, had gone to Bloomsbury Square and Bloomsbury Place, in search of Virginia Woolf. They were refused admittance to the British Museum, being under age, so they used their combined psychic powers to numb the minds of the attendants.

Through lunch, they talked non-stop about what they had seen in the Museum.

In the afternoon, they went back.

* * *

Aldous' only visitor was an eighteen-year-old girl, well-dressed, full of vitality, long blonde hair, wearing a very short, sleeveless shirt that did not cover her navel, with tight shorts.

She sat down and told, "My mum's very conservative, and well-off. To give you an idea, she doesn't like the way I dress."

"Indeed," said Aldous.

She grinned at him. "Do you object?"

"I find girls' tummies very suggestive," said Aldous evenly. "When they're flat and firm," he added mischievously.

He probed. She hoped not to pay in money but with sex.

'Please go on," he said.

"I was preggies when I was sixteen, and had to have an abortion. My mother never knew. You see, I've got two sisters, one like me, and the other uptight. So we're scared our mother could leave most of her money to the priggish one."

She pulled back her shoulders, thrusting out her breasts.

"And now the sister you like, she's pregnant too?"

"That's right!" said the girl, astonished. "She's got preggies, but she doesn't want to abort. With mother's money, she says why should she have to? I was thinking of telling mum that I was expecting too, but had to abort."

163

"Your mother won't allow either of you to go on living in the house. She has a cottage north of London which she'll offer you, with a tiny sum each week to live on. You are proposing to wreck her social standing with relatives and friends. Your rupture with your mother would be complete."

The girl looked stunned.

"What is my sister to do? Have an abortion?"

"I will give you the name of a Home for single girls who are expecting. It's the other side of London to where your mother lives. Tell your mother nothing about your own abortion. When your sister moves into the Home, tell your mother, tell her you are doing it to avoid involving your mother in a scandal.

"Your mother will be furious, but she will appreciate the thought behind your actions. Finally, she will come and visit your sister regularly at the Home, and help with adoption of the baby. Your sister will resist adoption, but she will have no option. Your mother will give no help to bring up the baby. Your mother will rationalise to herself that your sister has been seduced, foully seduced, that it's not really your sister's fault. You have a strong influence over your sister, and you must keep at her that she has to shut up, say nothing to your mother. Your mother will take her back. Living with your mother, you both will make comfortable marriages – I say 'comfortable' advisedly, in the sense of economically comfortable. Your children will be well looked after, and receive good educations. Your sister will fight every inch of the way, but she will listen to you, as she always has."

Soberly, the girl opened her purse and paid him. Aldous probed. No marked banknotes.

Walking her to the door, she began to cry.

"Do you want to sit down?"

"I'm all right, thank you."

* * *

Alone in the flat, Aldous paced up and down. What was Gulliver reading? What was he thinking? Would Gulliver explain anything when he came home? Aldous' mind felt in turmoil.

Annika and Jorge returned, and he was thankful for the respite they gave him. They chatted non-stop.

Gulliver came in. He was crusty, and ate his meal in silence.

Afterwards, he said, "Let's get out and have a walk."

They walked until nine o'clock. Gulliver's mood mended, but he was taciturn.

* * *

Next morning, Gulliver left with Annika and Jorge. The youngsters were eager to see the Tower.

* * *

Aldous' first visitor was at half-past-ten, and he forced himself to listen.

She was a plump thirty-seven, mother of three children, her face unremarkable but with shadows of discontent. Her breasts were large, and she made men aware of them in her light summer striped blouse.

"I'm married, but I don't have much of a relation with my husband. We don't really care for each other. I go to these evening classes in Art – drawing and painting. Well, you see, we have this nude male model who comes, and looking at his penis, I felt very disturbed. I became very conscious of the man working at his easel alongside me, so I struck up conversation. We went and had a drink afterwards, and I arranged to meet him next morning. I went to his house, and we made love.

"I think my problem is that I'm looking for a substitute for my father. My father made me feel very looked-after, and when he died, I went into a tailspin. I want someone who will love and protect me, but at the same time I need to dominate men, to feel I'm controlling things. It's as though I can't trust them to care and protect me, and I have to watch out. But when I control a man, I despise him, and I don't like men who I can't control.

"This man I met at Art school is very strong, emotionally, and he makes me feel secure, but I hardly ever see him. He calls the shots, and makes love to me only about once a week. I try to see him more often, but he makes excuses, and he never answers his phone. He always keeps his answering

165

machine switched on.

"Really, I'd like to separate from my husband, and I should have done it a long time ago, and I thought this man from Art School was the one..."

She smiled helplessly.

Aldous said, "He has two other girlfriends, who don't know about each other. He sleeps with one three days a week, when her husband is travelling for his firm. Then he sleeps with the other, also three days a week, and tells her he has to work the other days, or travel. She accepts this because he helps her financially, and because she has another boyfriend, who is finishing at University. These other two women are in their early twenties.

"You will never marry this man.

"You will separate shortly, and have the custody of the children. You will have other love affairs. One of your daughters will never marry, but will live with you for the rest of your life. Your daughter will become an accountant."

The woman looked at him, stricken.

Aldous smiled. "I have not given you bad news. After you are separated, you will be free of a lot of stress you now suffer. Many people are condemned to loneliness in their old age. You will have your daughter, and she'll bring her friends to the house. You will have other lovers."

The woman shook her head stubbornly, then opened her purse and paid him.

The banknotes were not marked.

Aldous probed further. The detectives had come back, and were parked near his building.

* * *

Aldous was edgy, thinking about Gulliver. When his next visitor came, he turned all his attention on her.

She was good-looking, sexy, and dressed with class, in pale greys. Her hairdo was expensive. She was twenty-nine, slim, with delicate hands.

On the chair, she crossed one beautifully formed leg over another.

"I've come about my boyfriend. He looks like a Greek statue, he has a Greek face with this aristocratic nose. People find him irresistible and I'm only happy when I'm in his company. People stare at us together. His body excites me because I fantasize having a lot of baby boys looking just like him. I tend to be a little morose by temperament; when I'm alone, I feel a bit down, but with him I spark up. He talks a lot, and everything he says is so exciting and interesting, I feel great."

"A match made in heaven," smiled Aldous.

"Well, now we've just lost a lot of our friends," she said worriedly. "He

166

makes friends easily, so we'll find other people. He persuaded my friends to pool their money and play the Stock Market. He says he bought these shares which dropped sharply in price, so he said we had better drop the whole thing, and he gave them back about a quarter of their money only. We didn't use a lawyer, and we signed no contracts, but he hasn't shown any paperwork of his investments. He was in and out of so many shares, it'll be a hell of a job tracking down what he did. He used different brokers and we don't know who they were. They're thinking of going to Court, but it's going to be expensive and incredibly time-consuming, and I've told them not to be silly.

"So – what will happen? As he is the man I love, I'm awfully upset and worried."

"They will not go to Court, because the search will be costly, and the lawyers much more. Your lover is a professional con-man."

She gasped, and rocked on the chair.

"He got into your group through you. He began working at this about three years ago, and has pulled a dozen scams. He's clever, and as you say, people can't resist him because of his extraordinary good looks and his charm and vivacity. Now he will gradually break off with you, slowly and carefully. You have about £15,000 he would like to get his hands on, but he realises it is too full of dangers. He now has to move elsewhere –"

Aldous smiled. "Move to pastures new, we may say."

"What will come of me? My God!"

"You will find another love, very soon, who will introduce you to a new circle of friends, but the two of you will finally decide to leave the city and live in a small village, where you will take part in all the village activities, and be able to go for walks in the countryside. Your £15,000 does have its compensations when joined to your future husband's capital. You both own houses in London, which you will sell."

She had turned deathly pale. She paid him with a tremor in her hands, and left.

The banknotes were not marked.

* * *

Gulliver arrived home shortly after Annika and Jorge. He looked worn and dispirited, and ate his lunch tiredly, with a few laconic words.

He went to an armchair, sprawled in it, and slept for twenty minutes.

He woke up, stretched vigorously, and said, "I have to report."

Aldous turned to his son and daughter. "He uses his watch to transmit to a robot hovering over us, which transmits... I'm not sure how. The message goes through another Dimension, through a universe parallel to ours, and arrives in no time at all at his planet. In our universe, the message would take thirty years to get there, because his planet is thirty light years away."

Gulliver made himself comfortable, took a deep breath, and spoke:

Urgent. Gulliver reporting:

Evolution on this planet has been torpid and parsimonious. Its progress has been slapdash, the labour of a dullard who believes a task to be impossible.

In the Forgotten Times, God sent wise angels to create us, and others of our group, to create the perfect beings that we are.

On Earth, from some unknown quadrant of the Galaxy, Very Superior Aliens have come opportunistically to Earth to play wicked games in Design – and what at first looks like the work of dullards turns out to be malice.

As natural catastrophes wiped out one savage wave of life forms, these aliens returned over and again to create more viciously advanced and depraved life forms, and for 500 million years did not bring in Intelligent Conciousness.

The evolution they have Designed is unforgivable, their evolutionary paths damnable.

Primitive Earth scientists believe some invisible chance blindly guides atoms to join up tiny accidental charges into the unbelievable intricacy of fantastic new life forms and their cells. Forms here persist millions, or hundreds of millions of years *with no change*, thanks to relentless DNA control, which kills deviants, making nonsense of Earth scientists.

All fantastic new life-forms come from the Aliens. Talk of tiny mutations shows pitiable ignorance. No one has ever found those intermediate fossils.

The first evolved life forms were unimaginative and defensive exoskeletons. Unbelievably, evolution built their brains around their gullets. The food channel runs down the middle of the nervous ganglionic matter, so if the brain is to grow, it must of necessity strangle the feeding tube and deprive the creature of food. For the creature to go on eating, its brain can't grow, because the tough exoskeleton won't let it expand outwards.

Your Excellencies will have trouble believing this, hut it would seem their amateur evolution was concerned only with survival and feeding, not with higher growth.

Blocked in this line of development, their evolution turned to the so-called creatures with a backbone – a hard inside skeleton surrounded by soft flesh and skin.

The first advanced creatures were reptiles. The vegetable-eaters had tiny brains, as their bodies grew more gigantic. These tiny brains guided them

168

to grass, plants and leaves on trees, and with this evolution was well satisfied.

Then it developed flesh-eating reptiles, with small, utterly ferocious brains – what I will call the Tyrannosaurus Rex brain. There were dozens of species of hunting reptiles – killers without equal. These came to dominate the whole planet for more than a hundred million years – and evolution rested *well content*, and sought no changes!

The environment changed – perhaps an asteroid impact in Mexico and in the Indian Ocean near the African coast. The change wiped out the reptiles, and allowed new forms to enter the continents – marsupials and placental mammals. The marsupial is less efficient, because the babies leave the womb for a pouch. The placental mammal gestates the baby much longer in the womb. It is born in a complete state.

With reptiles, a large part of the brain was taken up with the sense of smell. This was conserved, in the marsupials and placental mammals.

This parsimony in holding on to forms is carried to unbelievable lengths. Their reluctant evolution took a step forward, putting some creatures into the trees, where they were close to invulnerable. In the trees, sight and hearing are all-important, and in the mammal monkeys, the part of the brain given over to smell they shrank down to almost nothing, while the parts of the brain for seeing and hearing take up most of the space available.

In marsupials, that took to the trees, the huge part of the brain given over to smell is kept entire. It's useless for the animal up in the trees. The parts of the brain for seeing and hearing are relatively tiny, putting the tree-living marsupial in constant danger.

This mean scrimping is taken to unbelievable lengths. Five hundred million years ago, a new type of fish appeared. Before that, fish had fins, supported by ribs, something like a fan. The new fish had the fins supported by bones. Those bones are exactly the same as are found today in man, in his upper arm or upper leg, in his forearm or shin, in his wrist and ankle, in his hand and foot, and in his toes. All these bones were there in the fin of this fish five hundred million years ago.

The evolution of the fish diverged. Those with ordinary fins stayed in the seas and rivers. Those with the new fins finally came up onto the land.

Creating this fin was a creative act by the Aliens, but once done, they did not bother further. The bones are changed in size and shape for the fin of a whale, or for the legs of a horse, or for a hippopotamus' leg, or for the wing of a bird. But they are the same number of bones, in the same order.

Their lack of interest, of originality, of energy, their narrow-minded obsession with the Selfish Gene and with each creature gaining control of food while depriving others of that food, or killing them where possible, is shown in the development of the human skull, the apex of evolution on this planet.

Monkeys took to the trees, and became almost invulnerable,

developing opposable fingers and toes.

If we take a sheet of rubber, draw upon it a grid, and superimpose the drawing of a monkey's skull on that grid – and then stretch and distort the sheet of rubber, we find we have a gorilla's skull, with the same areas inside each square of the grid. Stretch and distort the rubber further – lo and behold! we have a human skull!

To hold the human brain, to contain a superior brain, requires a new form of skull, but their evolution did not build it. With incredible stinginess they developed the skull step by step from the old model, so that over four million years, pre-human hominoids had brains that painfully grew from 400 cubic centimetres to 800 to 1,000 to the present capacity of man today.

Evolution on this planet has been perverse and distorted, perhaps by the severity of conditions. But evolution has made the conditions far worse with the savagery of their creations.

After the age of the reptiles, they built mammals which lived in herds, in groups, with a dominant male or female... bison, reindeer, elephants, boars, sheep, cows... all in herds or flocks or packs, and each group with a leader. Monkeys and gorillas and chimps also live in groups, always with a top leader. They built a new brain for these creatures - what I will call the Bison Brain, or the Gnu Brain or the Cow Brain or the Dog Brain.

Man has inherited these brains. He has the Tyrannosaurus Brain and the Bison-Dog Brain. The first is a killer brain, the second a herd or pack instinct brain. These two brains are in man's archicortex, in his limbic cortex. 'Limbic' means 'shutting within a boundary', 'enclosing'. The lower limbic brain is the ferocious Tyrannosaurus Brain. Above it lies the higher limbic brain, the Bison-Dog Brain. Neither brain can use words, nor understand them. The lower limbic brain is governed by instinct, the upper limbic brain by feelings, especially feelings of herd or pack obedience, of belonging to the herd and destroying those who do not.

It takes very little stimulus indeed to fire the Tyrannosaurus Brain into instant ferocity and mad attack. Over some four million years, the Aliens have built the neocortex, overlying the primitive limbic brains, culminating in the large neocortex of modern man.

BUT THEY HAVE SLAPPED THE NEOCORTEX OVER THE LIMBIC BRAIN WITHOUT GIVING IT CONTROL OF THE LIMBIC BRAIN. THEY HAVE STUCK IT INTO THE SKULL BLINDLY, TO SERVE THE LIMBIC BRAIN.

Where other creatures have to use fang and claw, the neocortex can serve the Tyrannosaurus Brain with rockets and atomic bombs.

The leaders, the politicians, use the Bison-Dog Brain to control their populations. They are the dominant Bull in a herd of cows, and people blindly follow their feelings of herd obedience, as a dog follows its master. Their rational neocortex is good for nothing. In the advanced countries, the

170

Dominant Bull takes up to sixty percent of the national product. About one third is used for the old, for education and for policing. The rest is the preserve of the Dominant Politician-Bull.

This evolution, Your Excellencies, has been depraved – on this planet it has been depraved and perverse, and has produced a depraved and perverse race which is incredibly dangerous and threatening – the human, the Tyrannosaurus- Bison-limbic human, which cannot control itself, but is forever killing other humans, killing flora and fauna. The killing never stops, not one single day, and the Leaders are governed by their limbic brains – are irrational, ethnic, herd animal menaces.

As I stated, the Leaders take up to sixty percent of the wealth, and the citizens submit bovinely, dog-like. Twenty percent goes to the old, to education and to policing, but the rest could be employed in genetic research to drastically modify the human brain. Your Excellencies, this option is not even considered, because the very aberration of the brain, product of an aberrant evolution, precludes it.

As I understand it, only one world religion has promulgated these truths – Christianity. The Christians teach Original Sin - that, in effect, each baby comes into the world with a lower and upper limbic brain. They teach that a human from its inception is inclined towards evil. Interestingly, the Christian nations dominate the world and, with Christianity and its view of reality, have led humans to their level today.

Your Excellencies, the Betsabians – the UFOs as they are known here – suggest that when humans build the super weapons, they will exterminate themselves. These super weapons will pass into the hands of terrorist nations, terrorist groups, and fanatical individuals. Total destruction is assured within, perhaps, two thousand years.

I cannot recommend we establish contact with humans.

END.

"You're very harsh," sulked Annika.

Gulliver said gently, "Annika, child, I came here, in power, from the heavens, to judge the quick, and the actions of the dead, and I have weighed humans in the scales and found them wanting. This was the mission laid upon me."

Annika lowered her eyes, and. refused to look at him. Gulliver said, "Aldous, we should leave tomorrow, but I don't know where my scooter could land."

"I know a hidden field south of Appleby, in the north of England. It was a field to hide cattle from the Scottish Border raiders. Your scooter may have to hover at treetop level."

"No problem. We can lower the ramp for one hundred yards."

"I have a house very close to the track leading into it. We could take the train to Appleby, and rent a car. I don't want to take a taxi, because if we get out of the taxi on the roadway, we might be seen by people I know."

"Well," said Gulliver cheerfully, "In that case, why don't we go to the British Museum this afternoon? Who wants to go to the Large Magellanic Cloud without visiting the British Museum first?"

They drove out of Appleby on the Flake Hilton road, and shortly saw another car was following them.

They passed Mountfoot cottage, and Aldous saw faces at the window.

They turned into the track, and drove along it about two hundred yards, then got out and walked.

They bypassed the rotted barred gate, covered in moss, and walked on to the side track.

No one was behind them.

They picked their way along the narrow twisting track and stepped into the field.

Eric and Jocelyn were firing arrows at a target. They turned and saw Aldous and dropped their bows, staring unbelievingly.

"Daddy!" they cried, and raced towards him, flinging themselves upon him.

He embraced them tightly, then let them down. They were both talking at once, the words tumbling out, but Aldous held his finger to his lips. They fell silent, looking at him, and then at the other three, seeing the family likeness. They looked back at Aldous stupefied.

Aldous said not a word, but again put his finger to his lips.

Gulliver pressed his watch several times.

Gulliver, Aldous, Annika and Jorge stared at the sky, and Jocelyn and Eric lifted their gaze in puzzlement.

They looked back at Aldous, and hopped in frustration at not being able to speak.

Eric said, "Dad! Behind you. Who are those two men?"

Everyone turned around, as the two men stepped into the field and walked towards them. One of them pulled out his detective's shield.

He walked up to Gulliver as a disk appeared in the sky and raced towards the field. It hovered at treetop level at the far end, and a long ramp stretched out of it, like a poked-out tongue.

The detectives looked at it, and stared back at Gulliver.

"Who are you?" demanded the man with the shield in his hand.

Gulliver said, "I am he who commands unimaginable energies. You will never in your lives communicate what you have heard and seen, and are about to see."

The two men stood frozen.

Annika and Jorge broke into tears and embraced. their father.

Gulliver embraced Aldous, who began to weep.

Gulliver said, "Do you want to come with us?"

"Too many people depend on my money," said Aldous with a constricted voice. "Of course I want to come. More than anything else in the world."

Gulliver, Annika and Jorge walked across the field, through the grass, to the foot of the ramp. They stepped onto it, and it bore them upwards without their moving. They faced backwards, staring at Aldous.

They disappeared inside, and the ramp drew up swiftly.

The disk rose, undulating, its top side covered with coruscating light.

It rose higher and higher into the sky, then suddenly winked out.

Aldous stood with the tears coursing down his cheeks.

THE END